ANIMALS

'What's that?' Mandy as[...]

'What's what?' he repl[...]

Mandy's ears strained. It was a crackling, snapping sound, like twigs breaking. Mandy knew the sound well. It was the noise of her dad's Sunday morning summer bonfire – the sound of a surge of fierce fire as it destroyed the garden debris he routinely collected. Suddenly, her nose began to twitch. The acrid fumes of burning had rapidly filled the air.

James was standing statue still, a shocked expression on his face. 'It can't be . . .' he murmured.

'It is! It's a *fire*!' Mandy sprinted over to where the noise was coming from. The big barn! With her heart hammering fearfully in her ears, she flung open the door.

'Help!' she screamed. 'Oh, *help*! James! The animals!'

Animal Ark series

1 Kittens in the Kitchen
2 Pony in the Porch
3 Puppies in the Pantry
4 Goat in the Garden
5 Hedgehogs in the Hall
6 Badger in the Basement
7 Cub in the Cupboard
8 Piglet in a Playpen
9 Owl in the Office
10 Lamb in the Laundry
11 Bunnies in the Bathroom
12 Donkey on the Doorstep
13 Hamster in a Hamper
14 Goose on the Loose
15 Calf in the Cottage
16 Koalas in a Crisis
17 Wombat in the Wild
18 Roo on the Rock
19 Squirrels in the School
20 Guinea-pig in the Garage
21 Fawn in the Forest
22 Shetland in the Shed
23 Swan in the Swim
24 Lion by the Lake
25 Elephants in the East
26 Monkeys on the Mountain
27 Dog at the Door
28 Foals in the Field
29 Sheep at the Show
30 Racoons on the Roof
31 Dolphin in the Deep
32 Bears in the Barn
33 Otter in the Outhouse
34 Whale in the Waves
35 Hound at the Hospital

36 Rabbits on the Run
37 Horse in the House
38 Panda in the Park
39 Tiger on the Track
40 Gorilla in the Glade
41 Tabby in the Tub
42 Chinchilla up the Chimney
43 Puppy in a Puddle
44 Leopard at the Lodge
45 Giraffe in a Jam
46 Hippo in a Hole
47 Foxes on the Farm
48 Badgers by the Bridge
49 Deer on the Drive
50 Animals in the Ark
51 Mare in the Meadow
52 Cats in the Caravan
Hauntings 1: Dog in the Dungeon
Hauntings 2: Cat in the Crypt
Hauntings 3: Stallion in the Storm
Hauntings 4: Wolf at the Window
Hauntings 5: Hound on the Heath
Hauntings 6: Colt in the Cave
Ponies at the Point
Seal on the Shore
Pigs at the Picnic
Sheepdog in the Snow
Kitten in the Cold
Fox in the Frost
Hamster in the Holly
Pony in the Post
Pup at the Palace
Mouse in the Mistletoe
Animal Ark Favourites
Wildlife Ways

LUCY DANIELS

Animals
—in the—
Ark

Illustrations by Ann Baum

**Hodder
Children's
Books**

a division of Hodder Headline Limited

This book is dedicated to all my friends at
Hodder Children's Books – who have helped make
Animal Ark a very special series.

Special thanks to Ingrid Maitland
Thanks also to C. J. Hall, B.Vet.Med., M.R.C.V.S., for reviewing
the veterinary information contained in this book.

First published in Great Britain in 2001
by Hodder Children's Books

For more information about Animal Ark,
please contact www.animalark.co.uk

10 9 8 7 6 5 4 3

A Catalogue record for this book is available from the British Library

ISBN 0 340 78324 9

Typeset by Avon Dataset Ltd, Bidford-on-Avon, Warks

Printed and bound in Great Britain by
Clays Ltd, St Ives plc

Hodder Children's Books
a division of Hodder Headline Limited
338 Euston Road
London NW1 3BH

One

'I don't think I've ever seen *anything* so sweet!' Twelve-year-old Mandy Hope was kneeling beside a holding cage in the hospital unit of her parents' veterinary surgery, Animal Ark. She put the tip of her finger through the wire mesh. The tiny patient, a two-week-old fox cub, seized it and began to suck enthusiastically.

'You can't be hungry again!' Mandy said, giggling. She could see the swell of the cub's full belly, pink under a fuzz of grey-brown baby fur. Its tiny front feet paddled and pushed against the towelling bedding as it searched for milk.

'No more,' Mandy said firmly. 'There are jobs to be done around here, you know.' Gently, she extracted her finger. The cub began to protest noisily, making a sound that was halfway between a growl and a whimper. Mandy swiftly put her finger back into its mouth and laughed.

She loved Saturday mornings at Animal Ark. Both Mandy and her best friend, James Hunter, never tired of helping out in the surgery – either giving a bit of loving attention to the variety of animals recovering from operations, cleaning out the patients' pens, or preparing the feed. Today was a special Saturday. It was the start of the February half-term. Not only that, but during the night they'd had snow and, later, there would be a walk with James and his Labrador, Blackie, to look forward to.

The fox cub coughed, and gave up on Mandy's finger. It rolled over on to its side and tried to lick at the small, stitched wound on its tummy.

'Poor little Meadow,' Mandy murmured sympathetically. It was the name she had given the cub. 'You'll soon be better.'

The door from the reception area of the surgery swung open and James put his head round the door. 'Snow!' he began. 'Piles of it! Great, isn't it?'

'James!' Mandy turned to him excitedly, pointing at the cage. 'Just wait till you see Animal Ark's newest arrival!'

'What a tiny puppy!' James exclaimed, peering in at the small ball of grey fluff.

'It's not a puppy,' Mandy told him. 'It's a fox cub! I've called her Meadow.'

'Oh! Wow!' James pushed his glasses along the bridge of his nose and kneeled down for a closer look. 'What's wrong with her? Where's her mother?'

'A woman out walking her dog on the playing-field found her tangled up in the goal net. She must have been struggling for ages because it was wrapped tightly round her neck.'

'Ouch!' James made a painful face and took a closer look at the fox cub's throat.

'Then, my mum was feeding her with a rubber teat attached to the end of a syringe – and she sucked it right off and swallowed it!' Mandy explained. 'So Dad had to operate. He made the tiniest little cut along her tummy and pulled it out.'

'Is she going to be all right?' James stuck a finger into the pen, but the little fox cub had drifted off to sleep.

'Oh, yes.' Mandy smiled. 'She'll be fine. She only needed three stitches. Dad's going to ask Betty Hilder to look after her until she's strong enough to go back to her den.'

'Where is the den?' James asked.

'It was right near the goalpost, on the pitch!' Mandy said.

'Not really the most sensible place to make your home, is it?' James remarked. 'Never mind, Betty's had foxes to care for before. She'll know what to do.'

Both James and Mandy had great admiration for Betty Hilder. She ran the busy animal sanctuary in Welford, the Yorkshire village where they both lived. She worked hard to care for the lost, unwanted and injured creatures who came her way, bringing them in to Mandy's mum and dad when they needed expert attention. James was a year younger than Mandy, but he was equally potty about animals.

'You can always rely on Betty,' he said, adding, 'I bet she'll love Meadow!'

In her sleep, the tiny fox cub yawned, rolled over on to her back and whimpered softly. 'I think she likes the warmth of the infrared heat lamp on her sore tummy,' Mandy said. 'Oh, wouldn't it be great if we could *keep* her?' Her blue eyes were full of longing.

'Yes.' James was thoughtful. 'But you know she's going to grow up into a strong vixen, and she'd want to roam free. It wouldn't be the best thing for her.'

'I know.' Mandy sighed, pushing her fair hair behind her ears. 'Well, let's leave her to snooze and get on with our jobs. I'll start with poor George, the old Labrador with the broken knee.'

'Mandy?' Adam Hope was easing off a pair of rubber gloves as he came into the hospital unit. 'Can you and James run a couple of errands for me?'

'Sure, Dad.' Mandy grinned. 'Will they earn me a little extra pocket money?'

'Hmm, maybe!' Mr Hope tousled Mandy's hair, and looked in on Meadow. 'Ah, healing nicely – that's good.'

'So what do you want us to do?' James asked expectantly.

'Well, I've got a bottle of tablets for one of Betty Hilder's dogs – he's got arthritis rather badly. Will you cycle over to the sanctuary for me?' Mr Hope had started soaping his hands vigorously under a stream of running water at the sink.

'That would be great,' Mandy said. 'We were just talking about Betty!'

'No problem!' James nodded. 'We'll take Blackie for a run at the same time.'

Mr Hope looked doubtful. 'There's quite a covering of snow out there. We don't want any broken bones.'

'We'll be careful,' Mandy assured her father.

'Gran and Grandad could do with some help today, too,' he went on. 'They're busy getting ready for their big anniversary party and Gran wondered if you could pick up the invitations and take them to the post office for her.'

'We can do that!' Mandy said, smiling at James. There was nothing she liked better than a day crammed with things to be done.

'Your gran might reward us with some of her chocolate cookies,' James said hopefully.

'Yes, well, you'd better set off right away,' Mr Hope suggested. 'There's more snow forecast for the afternoon. Mum's been called out to an injured donkey and I've got a waiting-room full of people to see . . .' He trailed off, looking harassed. 'Where *did* I put my stethoscope?'

'It's round your neck, Dad,' Mandy said, grinning. 'Where it usually is.'

'Thanks.' He felt in his pocket and pulled out a small brown bottle of pills. 'These are for Abbey, the golden retriever. Give them to Betty, with my regards, will you?'

'Yep,' Mandy said. 'And we can tell her all about little Meadow, too. Catch you later, Dad.'

'I'll go and get my bike, and Blackie,' James told her. 'Meet you on the Green.'

It was one of those rare, beautiful winter days. The sky was a cobalt blue and the sun shone on the snow, making it extra-specially brilliant. Mandy screwed up her eyes against the glare.

'Wow,' she said, as James wheeled his bike towards her. 'Now I know why all those skiers wear sunglasses on the mountain slopes.'

James, muffled up in a thick waterproof coat, took a deep breath of the crisp, clean air. Blackie's tail whipped excitedly from side to side and he strained forwards to greet Mandy. He was restricted by the length of his lead, so Mandy cycled over to say hello before he pulled James right over.

'Right,' said James, tucking the cuff of his glove into his coat sleeve. 'Let's go.'

'Gran and Grandad first, I think,' Mandy replied. 'Then Betty.' She patted the bottle of tablets in her top pocket, just to make sure it was safe. James followed as she swung left, her breath frosting in the freezing air.

As far as she could see, away into the valley where the river flowed and up the other side towards the spread of the moor, the snow lay like a covering of cake icing. Welford was unusually quiet, for a Saturday. She spotted Mr Hardy, who ran the Fox and Goose. He was sweeping the snow off the steps to the pub's front door. Mrs McFarlane hurried by, wearing a bobble-hat and carrying a heavily-laden shopping bag. Mandy waved, and her front wheel wobbled dangerously.

'Mind how you go there, Mandy,' Grandad called from Lilac Cottage's open front door. He stooped to put out the empty milk bottles and sneezed violently.

'Bless you,' responded Mandy, coming to a stop on the front path.

'Morning, James,' Tom Hope said. 'Come in, the pair of you, and Blackie. Gran's made scones.'

'Oh, great!' James sounded pleased. He propped his bike against the wall and followed Mandy through the front door. In the warm hall, Blackie gave a mighty shake. 'Ugh! Blackie!' James scolded. 'I'm wet enough as it is, thank you.'

Gran was buttering a plate of steaming scones in the kitchen. The Labrador's shiny black nose twitched at the delicious smell.

'Just look at your muddy paw prints on my clean kitchen floor!' Dorothy Hope glared down into Blackie's pleading brown eyes. He wagged his tail so apologetically that she chuckled and shook her head, then slipped him a piece of scone.

'I'm up to my eyes,' she announced. 'This anniversary party is nearly upon us and I've *so* much still to do.'

'Well, we're here to help.' Mandy smiled, pulling up a chair and sitting backwards on it. 'Aren't we, James?'

James had his chin propped in his hands. 'Yep,' he nodded, his eyes glued to the scones. 'How

many years is it? Fifty, Mrs Hope?'

'Fifty, yes,' Gran nodded. 'A long time to be married, isn't it? Help yourself, James,' she offered. She had grown quite used to James's enormous appetite.

'How are the plans coming along, Gran?' Mandy asked, spooning strawberry jam from a jar on the kitchen table.

'Well, we've managed to hire the village hall for the night,' Gran began.

'And a band!' Grandad put in, from the door of the kitchen. 'Very smart.'

Mandy grinned. 'Wow! What about the food?' she asked.

'I'm going to do it myself, love – with a little help from my Women's Institute friends.' She smiled.

'Reverend Hadcroft has offered to donate a whole salmon, fresh from the river!' Grandad told them.

'Which is very kind,' Gran added. 'Only, now, I've got to find a fish-kettle to cook it in!'

'My mum's got one,' James said. 'I'm sure she'd let you borrow it.'

'Thanks, James.' Grandad nodded his approval.

'We're going to need all the help we can get!'

'Hmm, these are gorgeous,' mumbled Mandy, brushing the crumbs from the corners of her mouth.

'Well, now,' Gran wiped her hands on a tea towel tucked into the waistband of her skirt, 'these are the invitations I've done so far.' She picked up a pile of small white envelopes. 'But I don't want your grandfather going off to the post in this weather. He's got a cold coming and I need him fit for the party!'

'We'll post them for you, Gran,' Mandy said. 'We're on our way to the sanctuary to deliver some tablets to Betty Hilder.'

'Thanks, love. You are a useful pair! Have another scone each, and then you'd better go.' Gran was smoothing Blackie's glossy head.

'Yes, there's more snow on the way, by the look of it.' Tom Hope looked out of the kitchen window at the sky. It had a yellowish tinge to it – a sure sign of snow.

James helped himself to his second scone. 'Right, come on then, Blackie. Let's get going.'

Gran wrapped the pile of envelopes in a plastic carrier bag and tucked them into Mandy's coat pocket. 'Take care, both of you,' she said.

Mandy planted a kiss on her cheek. 'We will. If we're lucky, we might even get a mid-morning snack at Betty's house!'

'Cheeky,' grumbled her grandfather, scowling at her playfully.

James fastened the lead to Blackie's collar, then mounted his bike. 'Thanks Mrs Hope, Mr Hope,' he called, waving.

'Any time, James.' Gran grinned. 'Bye.'

'Ooh, that sky looks threatening,' Mandy remarked, as they cycled off down the lane. 'We'd better hurry, James, before it comes down in bucketfuls!'

Two

Having deposited Gran's invitations in the postbox, Mandy and James turned left and began to cycle slowly up the narrow hill road that led to the sanctuary. At the crest of the rise, James paused to let Blackie off the lead. He bounded away, disturbing the smooth, snowy contours of the field, his dark coat stark against the blanket of white.

'This should mean he'll run off his energy before we get to Betty's,' said James.

'Yeah, good idea,' Mandy agreed, watching the spirals of smoke from the cottage fires in the dale curling up out of the chimney pots. Blackie was a very friendly dog, but he was also energetic and curious – and there was no way of telling what kind of nervous new arrivals Betty might have in her care.

The Welford sanctuary had become the permanent home of a whole assortment of animals. There were dogs, cats, pigs, horses, donkeys – as well as the odd sheep and goat. Betty seldom turned away an animal, unless she was full, and she only rehomed her charges if she could be certain they would be properly cared for.

The descent to the sanctuary was slippery, and Mandy decided it was too unsafe to cycle. She wheeled her bike alongside James's, while Blackie loped next to them on the verge. His tongue lolled pink from the corner of his mouth, making him look as if he was smiling.

'Here,' James called, clipping his lead back on as they arrived.

At the start of the long drive to Betty's property, the five-bar gate was open. Mandy leaned her bike up against the fence and looked eagerly around the paddock for signs of any animals she hadn't seen before. She couldn't identify any new arrivals among the grazing sheep, goats and donkeys, but she could tell that Betty had been very busy.

'There are some new enclosures,' she said. 'Look, over there, and another over that side.'

'I'll bet she's getting them ready for spring,' James said, adding, 'Oh, there's Otis.' He pointed out the fat Vietnamese pot-bellied pig that Betty has rescued a while ago. He was rooting around, his snout in the snow. While they watched, the pig gave up on finding a tasty morsel to eat and shuffled back into the hut he shared with a few of Betty's chickens.

'Come on,' Mandy urged. She was beginning to feel the cold.

James steadied his bike and tugged on Blackie's lead, but the Labrador was rooted to the spot. He had stiffened. Mandy followed the dog's fixed gaze, and spotted a crouching figure, half in and half out of the door to Betty's big barn. It was a dog she hadn't seen before. It was glaring at them threateningly.

'James . . .' Mandy put a warning hand on James's shoulder. 'Look.'

The dog, a large mongrel, bared its teeth.

Blackie looked up at James, then lay down in a submissive posture.

'Good boy,' James murmured nervously, as the strange dog began to approach stiffly. 'Yikes, he looks nasty.'

Blackie's tail began to twitch hesitantly, announcing himself to the big dog as a friend. But Mandy's heart began to pound with apprehension as it stalked on with a particularly menacing look in its eye. It growled ominously.

'Betty!' Mandy called, but her voice sounded feeble to her own ears. She loved Blackie dearly. She dreaded the thought that he might be attacked.

'*Spike!* Here!' To Mandy's great relief, the loud, commanding voice had a miraculous effect on the dog. It spun round and trotted obediently back to the barn, from where the order had come.

'Phew!' said James, stroking Blackie. 'That was a close shave.'

A moment later, Betty stepped out of the barn and looked along the drive at the two figures near the gate. Mandy waved her spare arm and smiled. 'Hello, Betty,' she yelled.

'Oh, it's you!' Betty hurried forward. She wore

a hooded jacket and wellington boots and there was a smudge of dirt across one cheek. 'Sorry about that. He's a rescue, and he's still learning his manners.'

Blackie sprang up and wagged his tail happily at the sight of the familiar figure. 'He gave us a fright,' Mandy admitted, grinning.

'Poor Spike had been used as a guard dog at a factory. He was badly treated so he's become mistrustful of most people. He seems to think he needs to protect me from anyone who sets foot on my property as well!' Betty rubbed Blackie's ears.

'We've brought some tablets for Abbey,' James said. 'From Mandy's dad.'

'Oh, thank you!' A smile lit up Betty's face as she took the bottle Mandy handed her.

'You'll never guess what's come into Animal Ark, Betty!' Mandy began excitedly. 'It's the most adorable . . .'

'Sorry to interrupt, Mandy, but can you two give me a hand, or are you in a hurry to get back? I could really do with some help. There's no one else around today for me to ask.'

'Yes, we can stay for a bit,' Mandy said, looking

at her friend. James nodded.

'Right,' Betty was brisk. 'Earlier today, I had a load of logs delivered for the fire. Only, I was hosing out the duck-pond round the front at the time and I now see that they've been dumped right across the entrance to my garage. I can't get the car out!'

'We'll help move them,' James said, brightening. He looked relieved. 'I'm glad you didn't ask us to walk Spike!'

Mandy laughed.

'He's not a bad chap,' Betty said, shaking her head sadly. 'He just needs a chance in life.'

'Poor thing,' Mandy agreed. 'I'd like to meet him properly.'

'You will,' Betty smiled. 'But I've put him in the barn for now. Let's get to work, shall we? Then you can tell me your news.'

Mandy wriggled her cold fingers inside her gloves. She was looking forward to shifting the logs. There was nothing like a bit of hard work to warm you up! She walked with Betty past her small bungalow towards the single, ramshackle garage, which stood independently from the house. Blackie trotted along beside James, keeping a wary eye out for the big black mongrel. As they drew nearer the open back door, Betty's collection of adopted dogs swirled out to greet them.

'Hello, hello,' Mandy and James chanted together, stooping to stroke and pat them. Blackie was the centre of a flurry of sweeping tails and cold, curious noses, but the dogs knew him and seemed pleased to welcome him.

'Have you got any new arrivals, Betty – apart from Spike, I mean?' Mandy asked.

'Quite a few!' Betty sighed. 'Somebody brought me a lost cockatiel – he's absolutely beautiful!'

'Oh!' Mandy was thrilled. 'Can he talk?'

'Never shuts up!' Betty chuckled. 'He must have been someone's beloved pet, but he escaped and flew into a kitchen window and stunned himself. The man who found him brought him to me.'

'Is he all right?' James asked, frowning at Betty.

'He's fine – he's a cheeky little thing! You'll have to meet him before you go.' Betty said with a smile. 'And I've got a ferret, a new rabbit, another guinea-pig . . .' She broke off and pointed to the heap of logs, piled haphazardly across the entrance to her garage. 'Look at that!' she exclaimed. 'How can people be so stupid?'

'Gosh,' James commented, his hands on his hips. 'It's a good thing you didn't need your car in a hurry this morning.'

'Yes, well, the two men who unloaded them had driven off by the time I got back from the field or I would have made *them* do it,' Betty said grimly.

James unbuttoned his coat. 'No problem,' he said, playfully flexing his muscles. 'Where do you want them?'

'Under the shelter over there,' Betty pointed. 'Just to the side of the garage. All right?'

'Yep,' Mandy got to work. 'We'll have this lot shifted in no time.'

'You can let Blackie off his lead, James. I trust him not to cause any trouble,' Betty said. 'Now, tell me about *your* new arrival at Animal Ark.'

Mandy had a log in each hand. 'A fox cub!' she said triumphantly. 'She's only about two weeks old.'

'Just a single cub?' Betty asked, puzzled.

'Yes, she was brought in by someone who found her tangled in the net on the playing-field. The lady said there was a den nearby,' James explained.

'She must have wandered away from the den to

play and then got into trouble. Is she doing all right?' Betty asked.

'She's fine now. But she had a difficult start!' Mandy filled Betty in on Meadow's operation. Then she added, 'James and I thought she might have to come to you for a bit, until she's strong enough to go back to her family.'

'I'll have her here, of course, if necessary,' Betty smiled. 'You know me, Mandy, the more the merrier, if I've got enough space! And I've had the odd fox in my barn before, too.'

'Thanks, Betty,' Mandy smiled. She thought about Betty's barn. It was an ancient, rectangular structure once used for storing farm machinery. Its timber walls and sloping roof had had to be patched up over the years, but it provided the perfect winter shelter for Betty's family of animals. Inside, it had been partitioned off into pens, hutches and runs – and there was even a stable for Bubbles the pony. All the animals lived side by side, like one, big happy family. Mandy thought it was wonderful.

James was already working hard. He had shrugged off his heavy jacket and had perfected throwing the logs on to the grassy patch under the lean-to. Mandy tried to copy him, but the log she tossed missed its mark by a mile. She had to run after it.

'You two are doing a brilliant job,' Betty said approvingly. 'I'll leave you to it, and go and make us a hot drink, shall I?'

'That would be great,' James grinned. 'Thanks Betty.'

'Yes, thanks,' said Mandy, then she burst out laughing. Blackie had obligingly retrieved one of James's logs, brought it back to him and dropped it at his feet. He sat down and wagged his tail, expecting a reward.

James giggled. 'I'm not chucking these logs to amuse you, Blackie!'

Mandy straightened up. The heap of logs had been whittled down already. 'It's not taking that long, is it?' she sighed. She felt pleasantly warm from her efforts. She was just thinking about taking a short break, when she heard a sound that made her heart skip a beat.

'What's that?' she asked James.

'What's what?' he replied, in mid-throw.

Mandy's ears strained. It was a crackling, snapping sound, like twigs breaking. Mandy knew the sound well. It was the noise of her dad's Sunday morning summer bonfire – the sound of a surge of fierce fire as it destroyed the garden debris he routinely collected. Suddenly, her nose began to twitch. The acrid fumes of burning had rapidly filled the air.

James was standing stock-still, a shocked expression on his face. 'It can't be . . .' he mumbled.

'It is! It's a *fire*!' Mandy sprinted over to where the noise was coming from. The big barn! With her heart hammering fearfully in her ears, she flung open the door. Spike, straining against his tether, began barking angrily, his hackles high. Looking beyond him, Mandy could see that the timber forming the back wall of the barn was aflame.

'Help!' she screamed. 'Oh, *help*! James! The animals! Betty!'

'Fire!' she heard James bellow. As she hesitated at the door, she saw him run towards Betty, who was just coming out of the house holding a tray of cups. James waved his arms up and down frantically, and pointed. The little round tray went flying as Betty hurled it aside and began to run towards the barn. Mandy saw the china mugs splinter on the ground.

Inside, a fog of smoke filled the barn and stung Mandy's eyes. James hurtled through the door, pushing past her, and she stumbled in after him. Betty rushed forwards, falling to her knees in the straw beside Spike. Her face was grim and her hands shook as she fumbled to slip the lead from his collar. As the big dog raced out of the barn, Mandy's tummy tightened into a hard little ball of fear for Blackie. But there was no time to help the lovable Labrador now. There were too many other animals inside the barn whose lives were in danger.

With the back wall of the barn ablaze, the light was a peculiar, flickering orange, but through the haze of smoke the animals could be seen scrabbling frantically for their freedom. The sound of bleating, braying, baa-ing and whinnying in Mandy's ears was horrifying. She was desperate to help, but her legs felt wooden with panic. Where should she begin?

'Open the pens!' Betty shouted. 'Open up all the pens. Just let them get out! Hurry!'

Three

At last, a sense of purpose gripped Mandy. She had been standing, staring hopelessly at the blur of small furry bodies, as they tried to clamber and scramble to safety. If she opened the hutches and pens, she had reasoned, the smaller animals would scatter, never to be found again. Yet Betty, in her terrible distress, was shouting to her to do just that.

'Get them out of here!' Betty screamed again. 'I'm going to ring the fire brigade!'

Left alone, her heart thudding violently, Mandy suddenly knew exactly what she had to do.

'James!' she yelled. 'Over here!'

He turned, and she saw that his arms were brimming with three squirming guinea-pigs. Clutching at them, he blinked at her helplessly. His eyes were tear-filled with the smoke. Mandy heaved the first of a pile of light, wooden crates from the stack she had spotted in the corner. She tossed it to James, where it fell with a clatter at his feet. James seemed to sag with relief. He lowered in the squealing, struggling guinea-pigs who scampered into a terrified huddle in the middle.

'Good thinking,' he yelled, as he hurried back for more, almost knocking Betty over as she sprinted back into the barn.

'They're on their way,' Betty shouted, as she passed him.

Mandy lifted a second crate and dashed towards a straw-filled run. She scooped up the rabbits, holding them by the scruff of their necks and putting them down inside the box as carefully as she could. Then she ran back to the pens closest to where the fire had started.

Freed from their pens, the larger animals were making for the square of daylight at the big barn door. The clatter of hooves added to the noise and confusion. Betty was clapping her hands and shouting, 'Ya! Ya! Go on!' as she drove the bewildered creatures out of the barn. When Mandy looked up from her frantic work of piling the smaller animals into the crates, she saw that tears were streaming down Betty's cheeks and her shoulders shook with sobs. Behind her, the flames were reaching for the barn's timbered roof.

'Mandy,' Betty gasped. 'It's too dangerous in here. You and James had better get out.'

'But . . . the *animals*, Betty!' Mandy pleaded. 'You can't get them all out on your own. Let us help you, please!'

'They won't survive!' James looked stricken.

Betty looked around her at the terrible chaos.

'You're right,' she said, shaking her head sadly. 'I desperately need your help.' She reached out and snatched up a few smeared cloths snagged on a hook, used for polishing the pony tack. 'Here, quickly, let me tie these rags around your nose and mouth. And you'll take great care, won't you? If either of you start to feel dizzy or weak, get out right away!'

'We will,' Mandy promised gravely, as Betty knotted the strip of cotton sheeting at the back of her head, then reached out to do the same for James.

'What about you?' he mumbled through his mask. But Betty didn't reply.

'Right . . . hurry now,' she said. 'Piglets!' She pointed to the far corner of the barn.

Seizing another crate, Mandy hurried in the general direction of Betty's finger. It was difficult to see clearly, but she was certain that several of the pens she passed were now empty. The door to the last pen swung open but there, buried in a nest of straw, was a litter of tiny piglets. They were sleeping peacefully, a pile of pale pink-skinned bodies curled tail to snout. Mandy grabbed the first one to hand – and panic broke out. With a great deal of shrieking and grunting, they ran around in circles, their little tails whirring like helicopter blades. Mandy dived on them, one by one, and put them into the crate.

'Sorry,' she murmured. 'It's all right. I don't mean to frighten you. Really . . .'

The heat in the burning barn was overwhelming. Again and again she filled her crates and went back, raking through the straw covering the floor of the barn with her fingers and overturning the smaller hutches in a frantic search for any animals she might have missed. Mandy felt wet through with her efforts, prickling all over with sweat and trembling with nerves.

At last she stood up, and looked about for James. He was taking a moment to rub his eyes. 'I think we've got all the small animals out of their pens,' Mandy yelled.

'Yes, OK,' he shouted back. 'Let's start taking them outside now.'

Mandy staggered under the combined weight of the plump little piglets in their crate as she

headed towards the big barn door, into the open. The crisp, fresh air was a welcome relief.

James hauled several of the laden baskets to safety, and lined them up in the snow. Some of them began to shake as the frightened animals clambered for freedom.

'I think that's all of them,' James wheezed. He pulled the cloth from his face and began a fit of coughing.

Mandy, too, yanked at her mask, then breathed in deeply, drawing the clean, wintry air into her scorched lungs. She could smell the smoke on her clothes and taste it in her mouth. Gasping, she took a moment to look around.

It was an astonishing scene. Betty's dogs swarmed around the barn, looking scared and jittery. The sheep, goats, Bella the cow, Rosie the donkey and Charlie the ram were roaming aimlessly, keeping a wary distance from the burning barn. A bewildered muntjak deer limped away along the driveway. Cats had appeared, then scattered, taking shelter wherever they could. There was no sign of Spike, but Blackie, his tail tucked tight between his legs, kept as close to James as he could. From the many crates containing the smaller animals came the sound of squeaks and grunts and the scratching of little claws. The ferrets, Scamp and Susie, stood on their hind legs and peeked out. Their bright little eyes blinked nervously at Mandy.

'Oh, poor little things,' Mandy wailed. 'Where's Betty, James? Have you seen her?'

'She's gone back into the barn,' James said, comforting his dog with gentle stroking. 'She's having a final check . . .'

At that moment, Betty appeared in the door of the barn. Her face was blackened and she'd lost her woollen hat. 'Bubbles!' she shouted. 'Have you seen the pony? My Shetland?'

Mandy frowned, looking quickly at James. He shook his head, biting his lip.

'No,' Mandy shouted back. 'We haven't, Betty. Please don't go back in . . .' she pleaded, even though she knew it was no use. Betty would go back inside, in spite of the chance she was taking. She was that sort of person, and Bubbles was a particular favourite of hers. Desperate as Mandy was to see the animals safe, she could see the flames leaping across the roof of the barn now, and she knew it would be foolish to attempt to follow her. 'Please hurry up, Betty!' she shouted after her.

James looked ready to go after Betty to help, but Mandy stopped him. 'No! Don't, James,' she warned. 'It's too hot, and too smoky. It's really dangerous now.'

There was a sudden commotion behind them. Blackie jumped, startled, as a boisterous rabbit managed to overturn the crate he was in. It crashed over and rolled. In a minute, his companions spilled out and made a dash for the house.

'Oh, no!' James yelled, springing after them. The rabbits hopped away in all directions. Mandy, who was annoyed to find she was still shaking uncontrollably, made a grab for the long, lop-ears of a frightened female.

'It's all right,' she whispered, holding the trembling creature to her chest to try and calm it. As she did so, Blackie did something extraordinary. Mandy watched as the big Labrador tried to help James round up the escaping rabbits. He streaked after the biggest member of the group, which was making straight for Betty's open back door. When Blackie caught up with it, it froze in fright. He stood over the rabbit for a moment, his head cocked and a puzzled expression on his face. Then he simply lay down on top of it!

James hurried over. In all the drama, he had lost his glasses. 'Blackie? What have you got there? Let it go!'

'No, James, no!' Mandy shouted. 'He's holding a rabbit for you. He's being gentle.' She went over to where Blackie was guarding the terrified rabbit. His black tail swished along the ground, half triumphantly, half apologetically.

'Oh, good boy!' James said, peering between his front paws. Blackie had applied a gentle pressure to the rabbit's back by pressing on it with his chest.

'Clever dog!' Mandy breathed, seizing the rabbit with her free hand. 'We've captured all three. Let's put them back in the crate and weight it down with someth—'

From the direction of the barn, there was a splintering crash. Mandy froze and her heart somersaulted into her mouth.

'Betty . . .' She looked at James, who looked back at her, his eyes wide.

'Oh, Mandy . . .' he murmured.

Mandy dashed towards the toppled crate and righted it with her foot. She tipped the rabbits in, and James's foot went tumbling in on top of them. There was no time to worry about whether or not they would manage to get out again.

'Betty!' screamed Mandy, as close to the barn door as she could get. The fierce heat beat her back. Tears began to slide down her grimy cheeks. 'Betty! Where are you?'

Black smoke billowed out of the door. It was impossible to see past it. James was clutching on to Mandy's coat sleeve, his knuckles white. He seemed to be trying to pull her back, but Mandy wasn't going to risk going any closer anyway.

'Betty!' she screamed again, then coughed. Part of the barn roof had collapsed and from a jagged hole the tips of the orange flames could be seen licking towards the sky. The seconds ticked by like hours. Betty didn't reappear.

'James,' Mandy sobbed. 'Quickly . . . go and see what's happened to the fire brigade.'

'Don't go in there,' James looked up at her pleadingly. 'Promise?'

'*Promise!*' Mandy gave him a shove. 'Go! Quick!

Betty's door is open. The phone's in the little office.' James ran, with Blackie close behind him.

Mandy sank to the ground. Her fingers were bleeding, she noticed, from where she had scrabbled about in the barn looking for animals. Her chest was aching and she was trembling violently. '*Please*,' she muttered, 'oh, *please* let her be all right . . .'

Mandy stared at the smoking barn door, willing her friend to appear. And, as if in a dream, Betty was suddenly there. She was doubled over, coughing, as she staggered towards the open.

'Betty!' Mandy leaped up and grabbed her arm, dragging her quickly away from the barn. Betty stumbled along, then fell heavily into the snow.

'Bubbles,' she said softly, her head in her hands. 'I can't find Bubbles!'

'We'll find him,' Mandy soothed her. 'James has gone to ring the fire brigade again. Are you hurt?'

Betty didn't answer. She just kept shaking her head in disbelief. 'It's too late for that,' she said sadly. 'They're going to arrive too late.'

Mandy put her arm round Betty as she sat in the snow. 'They'll be able to do some good, you'll see,' she said kindly, though in her heart she didn't believe what she was saying. If poor little Bubbles was in the barn, his chances of survival were small. The tiny Shetland had been taken in by Betty when his owner's children had outgrown him. He was a dear little character, though very old now, and Betty adored him.

'The other animals are all safe,' Mandy told Betty. 'They're all out, safe and sound.'

'Thank you . . . so much,' Betty whispered, as tears began to slide down her blackened cheeks. Behind her, the barn was being eaten up by the fire and Mandy could see that it was breaking Betty's heart.

'They'll be here any minute,' James shouted, hurrying over. 'I rang them . . . they're coming. Are you all right, Betty?'

'My hands . . .' Betty looked down at her hands as if she'd just become aware of them. Mandy saw that big red blisters were forming in Betty's palms, and across her knuckles.

'Oh!' Mandy said, astonished. 'They're badly burnt, Betty!' She suddenly had an idea. 'I know! The snow! That'll soothe them a bit.'

Betty nodded. Then she coughed again, a wracking cough that went on and on.

They sat on the frozen ground, the three of them, in silence. As Betty put her hands into the snow to ease her pain, she cried softly. The dogs whimpered, cowering close to their beloved mistress, bewildered and afraid. And slowly, it began to snow. Big, soft flakes floated down and melted in the swirling, fiery air above their heads. Mandy hadn't the strength to get up and go indoors, and Betty and James didn't suggest it either.

Moments passed. From time to time, Mandy looked up, to see that Rosie and Clarence had wandered back towards the barn. In the distance she could see Otis rooting in the field and the dogs far away in Betty's kennels yapped and whined. Blackie sat close, huddled up against James.

When, at last, the scream of the sirens could be heard above the roar of the flames, Mandy's shoulders sagged and she burst into tears.

Four

Two lumbering red fire engines and an ambulance came to a halt in the drive.

'Over here!' James stood up and waved both arms above his head. But some of the firemen had clambered out and were already headed towards the little group huddled in the snow, some distance from the blazing barn.

'Anyone inside?' the driver called urgently, as he climbed down from the cab.

'No . . . humans,' Betty spoke through her tears. 'It's an animal shelter. We're missing a pony, that's all.'

The fireman nodded. Great black hoses were being uncoiled and dragged along the ground towards the flames. Mandy, gently hugging Betty, was very pleased to see an ambulance man hurrying towards them.

'Are you hurt, miss?' he asked gently, crouching down beside her. Betty blinked at him, as though she was dreaming. Then she began to cough.

'Her hands . . .' Mandy said. 'They're burnt.' Betty flexed her fingers and the snow fell away to reveal her scorched palms. She held them up for the man to see.

Mandy noticed that James was feeling around in the snow for his glasses. It was doubly important that he find them, so he could see, and so that together they could take care of all the animals. Mandy hardly dared wonder what had become of them all. The wail of the sirens had scattered them far and wide, and she was desperate to go and look for them – but Betty had to come first.

'Let's get you to the van, then,' said the kindly ambulance man, helping Betty to stand. She leaned up against him weakly as he led her to the waiting vehicle.

'Where will you take her?' Mandy asked, jogging

along at his elbow. Her legs felt hollow and strange. She couldn't tell if she were shaking with the cold or fright.

'Walton General Hospital, love. It's just a bit of smoke inhalation and shock and we need to treat her burns. Don't you worry now. They'll take good care of her there,' he promised.

'Thanks – both of you,' Betty managed, as she climbed into the ambulance. 'Ring your father, Mandy. He'll help.'

'Yes, I will.' Now that Betty was in safe hands, Mandy stopped worrying and her sensible nature rallied once more. She noticed thankfully that James had found his glasses. He was wiping the muddy slush from the lenses with his sleeve. Blackie pressed up against him, looking thoroughly miserable and confused. He tucked his tail tightly between his legs, as the ambulance reversed slowly out of the gate.

'Excellent!' said James in triumph, blinking happily as he put his glasses back on. 'Not broken.'

'James,' Mandy said urgently. 'Can you ring Animal Ark? Tell my dad what's happened and that we need help. I'm going to see what's happened to the animals.'

'Right.' James sped off in the direction of Betty's office, his Labrador close at his heels.

Mandy wondered where to begin. She found it difficult to drag her gaze away from the fire. Giant flames ripped through the roof of the barn, snapping the heavy wooden beams as though they were matchsticks. Firemen in yellow helmets swarmed about, grim expressions on their faces, as powerful jets of water from their hoses added to the noise.

'Keep back!' a man warned her. 'These timbers may topple.'

Mandy backed off hastily. 'Spike!' she said to herself. 'I must find Spike . . . then Bubbles. That's what I'll do first.'

The falling snow began to settle on her eyelashes and mouth as she walked away from the heat of the huge fire. Mandy skirted the bungalow, calling as she went. 'Spike! Here boy!'

She crossed Betty's garden, her eyes straining for signs of any of the sanctuary's resident animals. It wasn't too long before an ominous growling alerted her to Spike's hiding-place. The dog had crawled under a low stone bench alongside a paved walkway in Betty's front garden.

Mandy could see he was quivering with fear, and, as she came nearer, he backed further into his shelter.

'Nobody's going to hurt you, Spike,' Mandy said softly. 'You can come out, now. We'll go into the house.' She crouched beside him, remembering not to look directly at him, the way her father had taught her. 'You'll be all right, boy. Betty will come home soon.'

Mandy went on talking softly to the dog, soothing him with gentle words, until at last he poked his head out and tried to sniff at her. She

put out a hand, slowly, level with his chest. Spike shook the settling snow off his ears and nose, then touched his icy nose to her knuckles.

'There,' said Mandy. 'That's a good boy. Come on, now.' She was afraid to leave him, in case he ran off. But she didn't want to risk grabbing his collar and dragging him out.

'Mandy!' James voice was urgent. She stood up and backed away from the bench before she shouted back. 'Yes! I'm over here.'

'Your mum and dad are here – just coming in the gate. Have you found Bubbles yet?' James was hopping from foot to foot. His lips looked blue with cold.

'Wow, that was quick,' Mandy said gratefully. 'No, no sign of Bubbles, James. But I've found Spike. He's hiding under this bench.'

'Better leave him there,' James suggested. 'At least we know where he is. There are animals wandering all over the place!'

'I suppose you're right,' Mandy was reluctant. She felt so sorry for the bewildered dog. But, as she began to move away, Spike thought better of losing the new friend he had made. He popped out from under the bench and began to trot after

Mandy. When she stopped, surprised, and looked back at him, he gave a low growl, showing her his sharp white teeth.

'OK, I know you're the boss,' Mandy said. 'Just don't disappear, all right?' She walked on, and Spike followed.

'Dad! Mum!' she yelled, seeing her parents scrambling out of the Land-rover. Emily Hope's hands covered her mouth in shock as she stood looking at the collapsing barn. Adam Hope was shaking his head in disbelief.

'Mandy! James! Are you all right? How did this *happen*?'

'We're fine,' Mandy said, hugging her mother. 'We don't know. One minute we were clearing a pile of logs and the next thing, I heard crackling and smelled smoke.'

'Betty's gone in the ambulance,' James reported. 'She burned her hands.'

'Oh, poor Betty!' Mrs Hope put an arm round James and squeezed him too. 'Thank heavens you're both safe!'

'Dad,' Mandy urged, 'Betty's animals are straying all over the place. We got them all out of the barn – the small ones in wooden crates that we found – but some have escaped and we can't find Bubbles and . . .'

'Slow down, love,' Adam Hope held up a hand. 'One thing at a time.'

Mandy's father put a gentle, warm hand on her shoulder and Mandy took a deep breath. 'You've done brilliantly, both of you,' he went on. 'Tell me, as far as you know, are any of the animals injured?'

'I'm not sure,' Mandy shook her head. 'We had to bundle them up and push them into the crates as quickly as we could . . .'

'But we got them all out of the barn before the fire reached the pens,' James put in, rather proudly.

'Well done.' Adam Hope smiled.

'Bubbles is missing,' Mandy continued. 'And Betty was beside herself. It was when she went back into the barn looking for him that she got hurt.' She glanced behind her. Spike and Blackie were getting to know each other, though neither one of them was wagging his tail. One of the firemen came striding up to Mr Hope.

'Are you the farmer here, sir?' he asked.

'No,' Adam Hope said. 'My wife and I are vets.

The property belongs to the woman who has been taken to hospital. I'm here to see to the animals.'

'Ah, that's a relief,' said the fireman, tilting his hat off his perspiring forehead. 'There's a lot of them running about but we've checked in the barn and there don't appear to be any animals still inside.'

'Oh, thank goodness,' breathed Mandy.

'The fire's under control now,' the fireman went on, 'but there's extensive damage, I'm afraid.'

'How terrible!' Emily Hope still looked shocked. The drenched and blackened remains of the old barn gave off a mournful hissing sound, like a big, sad sigh.

'You'll keep well away, won't you?' warned the fireman. 'There's danger of the building collapsing.'

'We will, thank you,' Mrs Hope said.

'Right!' Adam Hope took charge. 'Mum and I will start by examining each of the animals in turn. James, will you go round to the kennel block and see if any of the kennels are empty, please?'

James nodded and hurried away. The holding pens were at a safe distance from the barn, so, although the animals were probably frightened by the commotion, none of them would have been harmed by the blaze.

'Piglets!' Mrs Hope exclaimed, as she peered into one of the crates. 'Where's their mum?' She turned to Mandy.

'I don't know,' Mandy looked miserable. 'Betty told us to open the pens to allow the bigger animals to get out. She must have run away.'

'They're too young to be out in this weather,' Emily Hope said. 'We'll need to get them into the warmth.'

'Oh, dear,' Mandy looked even more miserable. 'I should have thought of that. There was no time . . .'

Mrs Hope gave Mandy a hug. 'Don't reproach yourself,' she said. 'You've been wonderful.'

'I'm worried about Bubbles.' Mandy chewed her lower lip.

'Well, here comes James. Why don't you two go off and see if you can find him? He can't have gone far. Dad and I will see to this lot.'

'Kennels are full,' James reported. He was out of breath. 'Some have got cats in them, and there are loads of dogs. But they all seem all right – just a bit scared.'

'They'll calm down, with time,' Mrs Hope said. 'We'll just have to use Betty's kitchen as a temporary shelter.'

'Emily!' Mr Hope called. 'Over here! I think this cat has a broken leg.'

'Coming.' Mandy's mum hurried over to join her husband.

'James, will you help me to find Bubbles?' Mandy asked. 'It would be nice for Betty to know he's safe. He's her favourite.'

'Yep,' James shook the snow out of his hair and pulled up the hood of his coat. He took a moment to stroke Blackie, who still appeared very subdued by all the confusion. Mandy looked about for Spike. The big dog stood some distance away, but his dark eyes were fixed on Mandy as if his life depended on her.

'We'll be back, boy,' she told him. 'And so will your mistress, so don't worry.' She fell into step beside James as he headed down the drive.

The dogs in Betty's kennels kept up a loud and excited yapping as Mandy and James searched the tack room nearby for a headcollar and lead rope for Bubbles. As they turned left out of the gate towards the snow-covered hills, Blackie's tail began to wag briskly.

'Bubbles will be easy to spot,' James said. 'We'll be able to see his hoofprints in the snow, if he's out here.'

'Maybe, though the snow is covering our tracks pretty quickly,' Mandy replied. She felt worried. Bubbles could have bolted in any direction. The low, grey cloud and falling snow made it seem closer to nightfall than it was. Already it was hard to make out the individual trees standing on the hilltop in a dark and brooding clump. Mandy realised she had hunger pangs. The last hour or so had been a real effort and she felt drained.

'What time is it?' she asked James.

He hiked up the sleeve of his coat. 'Long past lunch-time,' he said grimly. 'I'm starving.'

'Me too,' Mandy admitted, feeling round in her jacket pocket for the odd sweet. She discovered an empty toffee wrapper.

'Here!' James exclaimed. 'Pony prints . . .' Mandy looked down at the ground. The marks were distinct, a semicircular stamp in the deep, soft snow. They led across the field and towards the thicket of trees.

'Thank goodness!' breathed Mandy. 'Quick, James, let's follow them. The snow is going to cover them up soon!'

Blackie entered into the spirit of the game and bounded along barking with joy, as James and Mandy leaped through the snow after the vanishing tracks.

'Hush, Blackie!' Mandy ordered. 'You'll frighten Bubbles.' And then her foot came down on something hard, hidden under a mound of powdery snow. Her ankle twisted and she pitched forward, falling heavily on to her right shoulder.

'Ouch!'

'What is it?' James half turned, then ran back down the hill to Mandy's side. 'Are you hurt?'

'I'm not sure,' Mandy said, wiping the snow off her mouth and chin. She flexed her foot inside her boot as gently as she could. From a distance, Blackie barked impatiently. A shaft of pain shot up her leg. 'A bit,' she said, in a small voice.

'Oh, Mandy!' James wailed. 'Can you walk?'

'I'm sure I can,' she smiled. 'I'll just rest for a minute, OK? You go on up the hill and into the thicket. Follow the tracks before they disappear.'

'Right,' James looked worried. 'Where are your gloves?'

Mandy looked down at her hands. 'Um . . . I don't know. I lost them. I took them off to move Betty's logs. Don't worry about that now! Just go!' Mandy urged him. She flexed her ankle a second time and winced. James hurried away up the hill.

Mandy could see a plume of grey smoke curling into the sky above Betty's barn. As she sat there, one of the two fire engines rumbled slowly out of the drive and turned right towards Welford, their work obviously done. She sighed heavily. There was so much to do, so many animals to find, comfort and shelter, and here she was sitting helplessly in the middle of a field in the snow. It was too much to bear. She struggled to her feet, putting pressure on her aching ankle.

'I've found him!' James yelled from the top of the hill. 'He's in here.'

'Is he all right?' Mandy shouted.

'Scared, but . . . I think he's fine,' James sounded uncertain.

'I'm coming,' called Mandy. 'Wait there.' She limped along, following James's footprints in the snow, trying to ignore the pain shooting up her calf. Her progress was slow, but Mandy was determined to make it. As she got nearer to the trees, she could hear James talking in a low voice to the frightened pony.

'. . . mints, and sugar-lumps, and perhaps a crisp, green apple, because you've been a brave boy . . .'

'Bubbles!' Mandy gave a great sigh of relief when she saw the plump, black pony. He whickered softly, looking back at Mandy with the fear of the fire still in his eyes. 'It's all right now,' she told him, smoothing his old nose. 'Don't be afraid. We're going to take you home.'

Bubbles seemed relieved to hear their reassuring voices. He stepped out from behind the solid trunk of the tree against which he'd taken shelter and snorted. Snow flew off his muzzle from where he'd been foraging for grass.

'Betty's going to be so pleased,' she said.

'Are you all right?' James asked, pointing to her foot.

'Fine,' Mandy said. 'I'm fine. Let's just get Bubbles back to the sanctuary and find Mum and Dad.'

Five

Bubbles meekly submitted to having his halter put on and being led out of the thicket. He walked slowly between Mandy and James, lifting his head from time to time to sniff the air.

'I can still smell the smoke,' said James, wrinkling his nose.

'I hope it won't make poor Bubbles too nervous,' Mandy said. She limped along beside the pony, stroking his smooth black neck, while James held the lead rope. Mandy wished she were able to go a bit faster. And then she had a thought.

'Of course!' she exclaimed, stopping. 'I can ride

Bubbles. I'm just about light enough, and Shetlands are strong. That way we'll get back to the sanctuary quicker.'

'But there's no saddle,' James protested.

'That doesn't matter. Here, help me over, James, will you?' Mandy grinned and raised her sore leg. Bubbles was a small pony, only about eleven hands high and Mandy knew that he was sweet-tempered. He made no objection to her sliding on to his back, only shuffled from foot to foot and snorted as the falling snow tickled his nose.

'I'm on, James!' Mandy laughed. 'You can stop shoving now. Ugh! It's wet up here! His back is soaked.'

'Come on, Bubbles, let's go,' said James. 'I'm about to faint with hunger.'

'Poor James,' said Mandy, as they set off. 'Phew! What a day this has been.'

They went on in silence. By pulling steadily on the lead rope, James was able to persuade Bubbles to move quite briskly. Lulled by the rocking motion of the pony's walk, Mandy couldn't stop herself from leaning forward, resting her head against Bubbles's dark mane and closing her eyes. She was achingly tired, but she knew there was

still a lot of work to be done before she could slide into her cosy bed in her room at Animal Ark. She must have dozed off, because she was startled to suddenly hear James telling her father that she had hurt her foot. Her eyes flew open. They were back at Betty's sanctuary.

'I'm fine, Dad,' she said quickly, sitting up.

'We'll see. But well done both of you for tracking down old Bubbles,' Adam Hope said, as he slid his arms round his daughter. 'James, will you tether the pony in the garage for now, please?' He carried Mandy in his arms, and strode towards the kitchen. 'Now, let's take a look at that foot, shall we?'

'There's nothing to look at,' Mandy said stubbornly, hoping she wasn't going to be told she would have to rest. Looking over her father's shoulder, she saw that some of the firemen were still prowling around in the skeleton of the barn, and noticed that all of the crates she and James had filled with animals had gone from the spot where they'd left them.

'Where's Mum?' Mandy asked, as her father lowered her on to the pine top of the big kitchen table.

'Down in the kennels, last time I saw her,' Mr Hope replied. He removed Mandy's boot, and her thick sock. A blueberry-coloured bruise had spread across her instep.

'Food!' James cried, coming into the kitchen. A chocolate cake with creamy icing lay on a plate on a worktop. His eyes fixed on it longingly.

'Tuck in, James,' Adam Hope chuckled. 'I presume it was meant for Betty's tea but it's unlikely that she'll be back for that. Does this hurt?' He pressed Mandy's foot.

'No,' she shook her head.

'What about here . . . any pain?'

'Ow! Yes!' Mandy flinched.

'Well,' said her father, when the examination was finished, 'I don't think you've broken anything. Just a sprain. I'll use some of my horse bandages to strap it up for you.'

'Thanks, Dad,' Mandy smiled. 'Can I have a piece of that cake too, James?'

'What's happened to all the animals?' James mumbled, his mouth full. He cut Mandy an enormous slice of the cake, then licked the icing off his fingers.

'Emily and I are using Betty's utility room as a

temporary shelter for some of them. And we've taken a few of them down to the kennels,' Mr Hope began.

'Spike!' said Mandy suddenly, interrupting. 'Dad, have you seen a light brown mongrel?'

'Yes, I think I did. Under a bench in the garden,' he replied. 'Seemed reluctant to come out.'

The door to the kitchen opened and Blackie sprang up to greet Emily Hope. Her auburn hair had come loose and was streaming down her back. Little flakes of melting snow clung there, glistening like crystals.

'Hello, you two. Hello, Blackie. I see you found Bubbles. Good work . . . oh! Mandy, what *have* you done to your foot?' Mrs Hope bent to peer at her daughter's ankle.

'Just a sprain, I reckon,' Adam Hope reported, as he uncoiled a strip of bandage.

'I tripped,' Mandy told her mother. 'But I'm fine. How are all the animals?'

Mrs Hope slipped an arm round Mandy's shoulders. 'We've rounded nearly all of them up, and there don't seem to be any serious injuries so far.'

'One cat with a broken leg,' Adam Hope put in.

'Yes. You know, I think it was up on the roof of the barn when the fire broke out. It must have jumped, and landed badly,' Emily Hope said, adding, 'Fractures are quite rare in cats.'

'What are we going to do now?' asked James, who was sitting cross-legged on the kitchen floor. 'With all the animals I mean?'

Mrs Hope looked at her husband. He finished tying Mandy's bandage and stood up.

'I'm not really sure . . .' he frowned. 'Any ideas, Emily?'

Mrs Hope opened her mouth to speak, but her voice was drowned out by the sound of excited barking. Betty's pet dogs were making a fuss on the driveway outside. James jumped up and looked out.

'Oh!' he said. 'There are a load of people milling around staring at the barn and . . .'

'It's Simon! And Jean . . . and Ernie Bell,' Adam Hope had joined James at the window. 'It looks like people from the village have turned out to help. Go on, Emily, open the door!'

Simon, Animal Ark's veterinary nurse, was first into the kitchen. He was carrying a couple of wire cages stuffed with veterinary supplies. 'Anybody hurt?' he asked, looking around.

Mandy grinned at him as she rolled her sock over her bandaged foot. 'Nothing we can't handle,' she said, pleased to see him.

'Good of you to come,' Adam Hope said. 'Hello Ernie . . . Jean . . .'

'It was quiet in the surgery, so we closed a bit early to see if there's anything we could do to help,' Jean Knox, the surgery receptionist, explained. 'News of this fire is racing around the village, I can tell you! How's Betty?'

'She's going to be fine. They're checking her over at the hospital,' Emily Hope said.

Jean Knox blinked at Mrs Hope through her glasses. 'Tea!' she said, filling Betty's kettle and finding the teapot. 'I'm sure you could do with a nice hot cup!'

'Ah!' Mandy's mum smiled. 'You're an angel, Jean!'

'Them animals is making a devil of a fuss in that room.' Ernie Bell put his old grey head round the door. 'Looks like they want to get out!'

'They probably do!' Adam Hope smiled. 'We

haven't decided just *where* to put them all, Ernie, that's the problem.'

'Where are you keeping them now?' Simon asked.

'There's a utility room near the garage,' Mrs Hope explained. 'And some have had to double up in the kennels at the bottom of the drive. They're dry, and they're secure, so that's a start.'

Mandy put her foot down carefully and eased her weight on it. There was far less pain than before it had been bandaged. 'I'm going to get Spike to come in, if I can,' she announced, looking out at the snow.

'What shall we do, Adam?' Jean Knox asked.

'Well . . .' he began, but he was interrupted.

'I'll feed some of 'em,' Ernie decided. 'I'm good at that.'

'Ah, well, I don't think we'll worry about feeding just now, Ernie. Housing is what we . . .'

'*Hellooo!*' The lilting greeting floated in through the kitchen door. Mandy saw her parents exchange a look.

'It's Mrs Ponsonby!' said James. 'I'd recognise that "Hellooo" anywhere.'

Jean Knox opened the door. The elderly visitor

was flushed and breathless. Layers of warm clothing had swelled her to double her size. She squeezed into the cramped kitchen.

'My dear! I came as soon as I heard. What a dreadful business! Is there something I can do? Of course, I've had to leave Pandora at home, with Toby. My poor little girl was terribly distressed to be abandoned but, I know my duty and . . .'

'Hello, Mrs Ponsonby,' Mandy interrupted her cheerfully. There were far more important things to be done than to hear the endless tales about fussy Mrs P's spoiled Pekinese. 'Come in and have a cup of tea.'

'*Isn't* it filthy weather?' grumbled the old lady, peering anxiously at Mrs Hope. 'You're not hurt, are you, dear?'

'No one is seriously hurt,' smiled Mrs Hope. 'Actually, Adam and I got here after Betty, James and Mandy had pulled all the animals out of the burning barn to safety . . .'

'Oh! Well done, my dears! How splendid! How brave!' Mrs Ponsonby found a chair and gratefully accepted the cup of tea Jean handed her.

'More people arriving,' James reported from

his stance at the window. 'Reverend Hadcroft . . . Mr and Mrs Hardy . . .'

Adam Hope flung the door wide. 'Come in!' he called. 'We're all in here. Welcome.'

In minutes, Betty's small kitchen was overflowing with concerned Welford residents. A steady trickle of villagers hurried up the snowy drive to the house, bringing boxes, blankets, towels and tins of food. Ted Forrester, the local RSPCA inspector, had even brought a bale of straw. Mandy was pressed up against the cooker, her escape blocked by people crowding in the door.

'It's so good of you all to come,' Mr Hope began. 'Betty Hilder has been taken into hospital. We've been told she isn't seriously hurt but, as you have seen, the barn she was using to house her many animals has been destroyed by the fire.'

'What about the kennels? Could we use them as an emergency measure?' Ted Forrester asked.

'We've doubled up, where possible, on the available space already,' said Mrs Hope.

'I'll come up and feed the animals here at the sanctuary, for the time being,' Ernie Bell said again. 'I'll make sure they're all right – them lot down in the kennels, I mean. It's them in that *room* you want to be thinking about.'

'Yes, you're right, Ernie,' Adam Hope agreed. There was a buzz of conversation and he raised his voice to be heard. 'We'll need volunteers. Will you all please just take a walk around, keeping a careful eye out for any animal that might have escaped our notice? And if anyone can give an animal a temporary home, we'd be very grateful.'

'What about us?' Mandy hissed.

Mrs Hope turned to her. 'Mandy, love, Animal Ark is full to bursting!'

'Not in the cottage, it's not,' replied Mandy. Her eyes were wide with longing. 'Can we? Take some of the animals in, I mean?'

'Let's see how we go, shall we?' Emily Hope was guarded. Mandy was aware of how well her mum knew her. She would have had the cottage attached to the surgery filled to the rafters with creatures of every kind, at the drop of a hat.

'Mrs Hope?' Sara Hardy called from the door. 'Here's Lydia Fawcett – and Adam's parents.'

'We'd better get out of this kitchen!' Mandy's

mother suggested. 'If we squeeze any more people in here, the house might fall down – and that's all we need!'

Neighbours, friends and clients of Adam and Emily Hope spread out around the grounds of Betty's bungalow. James was dispatched to the kennels to distribute fresh straw to the new residents, while Mandy went off in search of Spike. She was passing the open window to the sitting room when she distinctly heard somebody talking.

'Very pretty,' said a voice. 'Very, very pretty!'

Mandy stood on tiptoes and looked through the window. It sounded like a child's voice. Puzzled, she looked round the empty room.

'Good Jazz. Oh, what a good boy! Hello!'

'Hello,' replied Mandy politely, wondering who on earth she could be talking to. And then she burst out laughing. A small white cockatiel was perched on the back of a chair.

'Hello!' it said again, fixing beady little eyes on her and cocking its head. It had a bright yellow face and splashes of red on its cheeks.

'Wow!' Mandy breathed. 'Aren't you gorgeous? You must be the cockatiel Betty was telling us about.' The bird shuffled along the back of the chair, blinking at her comically.

'Very pretty,' it said.

Mandy giggled. 'I'll come back for you in a while,' she told the bird. 'I won't forget about you.'

'Have a tomato!' shouted the cockatiel, as Mandy drew away from the window. Betty really was an amazing person to be able to care for such a wonderful variety of animals, she reflected. Perhaps, when she had qualified from university with a degree in veterinary medicine, she too would run a sanctuary just like this one.

Spike was still under the stone bench. He pricked up his ears when he saw Mandy.

'Here I am, boy,' she said gently. 'Why don't you come on inside now and get warm? Slowly, Mandy put out her hand and the big dog sniffed at her carefully. 'Come on, Spike. Good boy,' Mandy said. She began to walk away, and, once again, hesitantly at first, Spike followed.

Mandy's parents were pairing off volunteer-carers with Betty's homeless animals. Walter Pickard had arrived, and a policeman was stalking around the shell of the barn writing in a small notebook.

'Mum!' Mandy said excitedly. 'There is the most wonderful cockatiel in Betty's sitting-room!'

'Oh, no,' Mrs Hope groaned. 'Not another creature to find a home for.'

'I'll take the cockatiel,' Grandad put in quickly, 'I'm fond of birds. They don't need walking! You all right, love?' he asked Mandy.

'I'm fine,' Mandy assured him. She was enormously relieved now that plans were being made for the sanctuary animals.

Julian and Sara Hardy had immediately offered to house Betty's four adopted dogs and Reverend Hadcroft was keen to care for some of the guinea-pigs.

'Cats?' Emily Hope called. 'Anyone for the cats? There are seven of them . . .'

'Cats are too difficult to uproot,' Lydia Fawcett protested. 'Really they are.'

'Well, the cats can stay here,' Mr Hope suggested. 'You're right. They'll be better off staying where they are. Will anyone volunteer to come down and feed them?'

'I'll do the feeding,' Ernie Bell said again. 'I told you that. Walter will help me. We'll feed and water the animals that stay put, won't we, Walter?'

'Aye, we will,' Walter nodded, but he looked bemused.

'Gran and I will take the goat – and the bird,' Grandad said.

'Now just a minute there, Tom,' Dorothy Hope scolded. 'That goat has a *kid*, you know!'

'It won't be any trouble,' Grandad was firm. 'I'll look after it. We can't separate mother and child now, can we?'

'I suppose not,' she agreed, looking reluctant. 'Where are we going to put them?'

'The shed will do,' Grandad grinned. 'I'll give it a clean out. It's big enough – warm too. And I'll make sure they stay away from your precious garden.'

Gran didn't look convinced, Mandy thought. She had been trying to get a word in edgewise and was almost bursting to know whether her parents would allow her to take a few of the animals into their own home.

'Spike . . .' she managed. 'The sad-looking black mongrel – over there . . .' Everyone turned to look where Mandy was pointing. Spike kept his distance, his anxious eyes on Mandy. 'Can I at least look after him, *please*?'

Before her mum and dad could reply, Mrs Ponsonby spoke up. 'I suppose *I* could take an animal in . . . just one, mind. I don't want Pandora getting upset. She's so much more sensitive than Toby. But I think I'll take that gerbil, the little cream one, over there . . .'

'I'll look after Bubbles,' Ted Forrester said. 'He'll need proper stabling in this weather.'

The chorus of bidding grew louder, until Mandy thought she would explode with impatience. And then Mrs Hope came over to her side.

'Dad and I have decided,' she whispered. 'You can bring home the animals we can't find homes for today. We'll all muck in, just until Betty is back on her feet, OK?'

Mandy flung her arms around her mother. '*Thanks*, Mum,' she said, her eyes shining. 'Oh, thanks!'

Six

Back at Animal Ark, Mrs Hope persuaded Mandy to have a hot bath and a proper meal before she did anything else. Although she tried to protest, she was really quite grateful for both. She was torn between a longing for sleep, and a wish to see Betty's animals happily settled in her own home.

'I'll keep an eye on them all,' her mother promised. 'You go and take care of yourself – for a change!'

Mandy could hardly believe the amazing turn the day had taken. It had started out ordinarily enough – and now she was the foster-carer to a large lop-eared rabbit, two guinea-pigs, a pair of ferrets, several hamsters, a baby chinchilla, and a large dog.

Coming into the cosy kitchen, wrapped in her dressing-gown and wearing thick socks, Mandy was happy to see Spike lying under the kitchen table. She crouched down, but didn't try to touch him. He still had a wary expression in his eyes.

'Good boy! You see, I told you, nobody's going to hurt you,' she said softly.

'He's a darling,' Emily Hope said, putting a plate of scrambled eggs on toast in front of Mandy. She drew the kitchen curtains, blotting out a gloomy grey sky that was still heavy with snow. 'All he wants is a chance to trust people again.'

'Did Dad ring the hospital?' asked Mandy, tucking in to her supper.

'Yes. Betty's going to be fine. They're treating her for smoke inhalation and burns to her hands. She should be home in a couple of days.'

'Can we go and see her? I'll bet she'll want to know about the animals,' Mandy said.

'I don't see why not.' Emily Hope smiled. 'You and James are going to be celebrities after what you did at the sanctuary today. I'm sure Betty would like a chance to thank you.'

'Poor Betty. I wonder what she'll do now that she hasn't got a barn to keep her animals in?' Mandy said.

'Oh, I'm sure there won't be a problem,' replied Mrs Hope, handing Mandy a glass of milk. 'Betty will have had the barn insured. The fire was an accident, and so the company she's insured with will give her some money to have it rebuilt.'

'Oh, good.' Mandy grinned. 'Then, can we keep the animals here until it's finished?'

'Hmm, I suppose so!' Mrs Hope laughed. 'This house is *stuffed* with animals, Mandy! It's what you've always wanted!'

'You're right!' Mandy smiled. 'It's a dream come true.'

By the time they had closed the gates to the sanctuary, all of the animals had been found temporary homes. Those remaining behind had been left in the capable hands of Ernie Bell and Walter Pickard.

Mrs Ponsonby had been the first to drive away, clutching a shoebox containing her single gerbil as though she had been entrusted with the crown jewels. It had taken Gran and Grandad nearly an hour to persuade the cockatiel back into his cage, and Gran had a fit of the giggles at the things the bird could say.

'Open the door!' he squawked, as Grandad thrust him into the car. 'You're a pretty boy.'

Lydia Fawcett, the owner of High Cross Farm, had provided transport for the larger animals. She had, at first, tried to persuade Grandad that the goat and her kid could more easily be kept at her farm, but Grandad insisted that he and Gran do their bit to help Betty. So Lydia delivered the female goat and her tiny kid to Lilac Cottage, and helped Tom Hope to set up a temporary shelter in the garden shed.

Jack Mabson, the dairy farmer at Baildon Farm, had taken in the little muntjak deer along with Otis, Betty's huge pot-bellied pig, whose sty had been turned over to a ewe with her newly-born twin lambs.

Publicans Sara and Julian Hardy had crammed Betty's four dogs into the back of their car and set off back to the Fox and Goose accompanied by a volley of hysterical barking. Simon carried the cat with the broken leg back to the hospital unit at Animal Ark and Jean had given a home to a pair of rabbits and three hamsters.

'What became of Bubbles in the end?' Mrs Hope asked Mandy. 'In all the confusion, I seem to have lost track of him.'

'Mr Forrester said he would need proper stabling. He said he'd get it organised and come back for Bubbles later,' Mandy said.

'I think you're going to need James's help with the animals you have right here,' Emily Hope glanced at the big dog under the table. 'Spike will need settling . . . and walking . . . and that's just the *start* of it!'

'Yep, that's just what James and I decided.' Mandy smiled. She took her plate to the sink to rinse it. 'Thanks, Mum, that was delicious. I'm going to go and see to all the animals now.'

'How's your ankle?' Mandy's mum asked.

'It feels better already.' Mandy grinned. 'Really, I'm fine.'

'Well, take care of it,' she ruffled Mandy's hair. 'And shout if you need my help.'

'I will. Coming, Spike?' He put his head out from under the table, sizing up the room for signs of danger before he ventured out. Then, very hesitantly, he went after Mandy.

First, Mandy raided the storeroom at Animal Ark for supplies. Her dad had suggested she help herself to the things she needed for feed and bedding while he operated on the leg of Betty's cat. It was great fun being able to rummage around in the surgery's big cupboard and make a pile of the packets and tins.

She began with Spike. Feeding him a delicious meal, Mandy reasoned, was a sure way to get him to see that she meant him no harm. The big dog went eagerly to his bowl, then snatched a bite and stood back, cowering nervously while he ate. When Mandy tried to soothe him with a stroke, he showed her his teeth. But Mandy refused to be discouraged. She was certain she would win him over in the end.

Upstairs in the spare room, spread along the newspaper-covered floor, were the cages of her various charges. They blinked up at her and scurried frantically in the sudden glare of the electric light. 'Poor things,' Mandy said. 'You've had enough of a scare for one day!'

Carefully, she freshened the bedding of each animal in turn, then sought out containers to use for water and measured out the correct quantities of feed into bowls. She was particularly thrilled by the chinchilla, who watched her with curious, dark eyes. Mandy wished that she knew where each of the animals had come from and what Betty had named them.

She was just about to lift the lop-eared rabbit for a cuddle, when the telephone rang. Mandy waited, hoping her mother would pick it up. After the fourth ring, she heard Mrs Hope shout, 'I'm in the bath, Mandy! Can you get it?' And she hobbled down the stairs and grabbed the receiver.

'Hello?'

'Is that you Mandy?' said a voice.

'Betty! It's Betty, isn't it? How are you feeling?' Mandy was surprised and pleased to hear her voice.

'I'm OK . . . look, I'm phoning from the public call box here in the hospital and I haven't any more change, so I'll talk quickly,' Betty said.

'Right,' replied Mandy, holding the phone nearer her ear and listening intently.

'Your father rang – he said all of the animals

had been successfully rounded up. Thanks! But, did you, by any chance, come across my tortoise?' she asked.

'A tortoise!' Mandy repeated. 'Um . . . no, Betty. We didn't know there was one! Where was he?'

'Well, Timothy's hibernating at the moment. I put him in a small cardboard box in the lean-to next to the garage. I'm worried about him because the heat of the fire might have . . .'

The phone went dead and Mandy was left frowning at the receiver. Betty's money had run out.

'Oh, dear,' said Mandy. 'Poor *tortoise!*'

'What is it, love?' Mrs Hope appeared at the top of the stairs in her dressing-gown, her hair in a towel wrapped like a turban.

'Oh, Mum!' Mandy wailed. 'That was Betty. She's worrying about her tortoise. She left him in a box, and nobody *knew* about him. He might have been disturbed by the fire.'

'That's quite likely,' Emily Hope frowned. 'It's best to check that he's safe and still asleep.'

'I'll go!' Mandy volunteered immediately. 'James will come with me. We'd like to go. Can we, please?'

Mrs Hope looked at the clock on the landing table. 'It's seven o'clock, Mandy – and still snowing. And you've got a bad ankle. You'll need a lift.' She sighed. 'OK, I'll go and get dressed and see what I can organise.'

'Thanks, Mum!' Mandy gave her mother a quick hug as she passed her on the stairs. Spike regarded her with anxious eyes. He lowered his head, his tail between his legs. Mandy wished she could reassure him. There had been little time to really get to know the dog. She would rescue Timothy – and then spend some proper time with poor Spike.

Emily Hope was saved the trouble of a trip out in the Land-rover by Simon's offer of help. Having assisted Mr Hope in setting the leg of the cat, he was just on his way home. He had gladly agreed to drive Mandy and James back to the sanctuary, so Mandy rang James, and told him about Timothy.

'Haven't you had enough rescuing for one day?' Simon grinned, as Mandy jumped into his car. She was muffled up against the cold.

'This time, it's a tortoise,' she told Simon,

putting on her seatbelt. 'Betty thinks it might have been woken up by the fire.'

'Tortoises occasionally begin to wake up around this time of year anyway,' Simon said, adding, 'Mind you, it's a bit cold still. I've brought my torch, so we can have a good search.'

'Thanks, Simon,' Mandy said appreciatively. She waved at James, who was waiting as instructed by the gate of his house. The car slowed to a stop, and he got into the back.

'I didn't know Betty *had* a tortoise!' he said.

'Neither did I,' Mandy agreed.

A full yellow moon was peeping through a chink in the clouds. The snow had carved contours on the roofs of houses and on the side of the road and Mandy thought it looked beautiful. She gazed out of the window at the fairytale landscape while Simon eased the car down the hill that led to the sanctuary.

A few moments later, Simon fiddled with the latch of the big five-bar gate, illuminated by his car headlights. Immediately, the dogs in the kennels began an agitated chorus of barking. Mandy hoped they would not frighten the animals who had been forced to share their block.

Stamping the snow from his boots and rubbing his hands, Simon got back into the car and drove up as far as Betty's bungalow. The ruin of the wrecked barn loomed large in the ghostly light, sending a shiver down Mandy's spine. It was a forlorn sight, standing there so bare and broken.

'Yuck,' James said, holding his nose. 'What a horrible smell.'

'Burnt wood,' Simon guessed. 'Not very pleasant.'

'We'll start by looking for Timothy in the lean-to where we began to stack the logs earlier today,' Mandy said.

'It seems like we did that a week ago now!' James chuckled.

'Yes, you two have packed a lot into just one day,' Simon agreed. He swivelled his torch and the beam of yellow light danced across the log pile.

'Just where did Betty say the tortoise was?' James asked.

'She just said he was in a box, in the lean-to thing – and then her money ran out on the pay-phone,' Mandy explained.

'Did you ring her back?' demanded James.

'No! I didn't,' Mandy was indignant. 'I wanted to get down here to find him as quickly as possible!'

'Well, we're here now,' Simon said soothingly. 'And don't worry – we'll find him.'

As they began their search, minutes passed in the icy darkness, but there was no sign of Timothy's box. The moon went in and darkness eventually enfolded them like a blanket. Mandy was grateful for Simon's torch. She moved her foot in a circle. The cold was making her ankle ache.

'Oh, dear . . .' she began, when James suddenly gave a shout. 'There's a ledge, up there under the roof!' James grabbed the torch and directed it to where he was pointing.

'That's a novel place to keep a tortoise!' Simon laughed, going over and reaching up. As soon as he had the box in his hands, it became clear to Mandy that Timothy had awoken from his hibernation. The sound of scrabbling and scratching could clearly be heard.

'Oh, poor thing!' she said. 'Quick, Simon, let's get him out!'

James shone the torch into the open box and

they all peered in. The little tortoise had been housed among shredded paper for warmth and was barely visible. But when Simon lifted his bedding, his scaly little head shot out, and his front legs began pummelling like mad.

'Whoa! Not so fast old chap!' Simon said. He put the lid of the box back on as quickly as he could.

'Do you think he's OK?' Mandy asked.

'I think he's been woken by the heat of the fire, and the smoke,' Simon explained. 'But I don't think he's damaged – just annoyed!'

'Let's take him home,' James suggested. 'Perhaps he'd like a drink, and something to eat.'

Simon entrusted the box to Mandy. 'Keep the lid on,' he warned. 'Tortoises can bite if they're alarmed.'

Mandy climbed into the front seat beside Simon. The clawing sound continued and her heart went out to the little reptile. 'What do tortoises eat?' she asked him.

'Bindweed and dandelion leaves mainly, in the wild, that is,' he replied. 'Timothy here may have a preference for something like lettuce or spinach – any greens.'

'Can I look after him?' James asked, from the back seat. 'I'm sure Mum and Dad won't mind. Only, you've got so many animals to look after now, Mandy . . .'

'Of course!' Mandy turned and grinned at her friend. 'You take care of Timothy. That will be perfect.'

'He won't be very pleased to be shut in that box, now that he's woken,' Simon told James. 'You'll have to keep him somewhere warm, where he can move about.'

'What about your little utility room at home?'

Mandy suggested. 'That's got a linoleum floor and a radiator too!'

'Good idea,' said James, sounding pleased. 'I'll shred some newspaper for him and make him a little nest.'

Mandy settled back as Simon pulled away up the hill back to Welford village. It was going to be a much busier half-term than she had anticipated!

Seven

Mandy had never known a busier Sunday morning at Animal Ark. It began soon after eight o'clock, with Spike demanding to be let out into the garden. Then James arrived, carefully carrying Timothy's box. He looked worried.

'What is it, James?' Mr Hope asked, stifling a yawn.

'He won't eat, Mr Hope,' James explained, putting the box on the pine table. A determined scratching came from inside. 'I've tried everything I can think of. But he hasn't eaten a mouthful.'

'Well now,' Mr Hope said, gently lifting the lid.

'That's not surprising, really. The poor chap has been rudely awoken from a deep sleep – to find that it's still *winter*.'

'But he must be starving!' groaned James, clutching his stomach dramatically.

'Not at all.' Emily Hope smiled. 'He'll need a few days to adjust, that's all. Don't worry.'

Mr Hope had just lifted the little tortoise to examine him, when the telephone rang.

Mandy made a grab for it. 'It's Mrs Ponsonby. She wants to speak to either of you. She says she's feeling alarmed,' she reported.

Emily Hope took the phone from Mandy and then spent the next five minutes persuading the elderly lady that it was perfectly natural for gerbils to shred their bedding, causing Mandy and James to collapse in a fit of the giggles. After that, the phone rang non-stop. It seemed everyone who had one of the sanctuary animals in their care needed help of one kind or another. Her parents gave up any thought of enjoying the Sunday newspaper and a pot of tea, and took turns patiently giving advice.

Mr Hardy then appeared at the back door, with one of Betty's dogs on a lead. 'There's been a fight,' he told Mr Hope. 'This one went for the collie and the collie got him by the ear. Will you take a look at him for me, Adam? Sara's quite upset . . .'

Mandy decided to leave her parents to it. She took James upstairs to see Susie and Scamp, the ferrets, and the chinchilla, whom she had christened Clarice. They sat side by side on the floor, watching each of the animals in turn. Spike stood in the doorway, his eyes locked on Mandy. He refused to come into the room or to sit down.

'Spike's still so nervous!' James remarked. 'Look, his eyes are all shifty and scared.'

'Dad says it's going to take him a while before he can trust anybody again,' Mandy said. 'I feel so sorry for him.'

She stretched out a hand to the dog. Spike watched her fingers warily, ready to spring away should she decide to strike him. But Mandy spoke softly, trying to encourage him to be petted.

'Good boy . . . nice Spike,' she crooned. She edged closer and tried to lay the palm of her hand gently on his head. He cowered, shivering, then jumped aside and showed Mandy his teeth.

'Oh, dear,' she sighed. 'Poor Spike.'

'Perhaps he wants to go for a walk,' James suggested brightly.

'Do you think he would?' Mandy's eyes were shining. 'I mean, go with us?'

'I reckon,' James stood up. 'I think he'd be really pleased if we took him out.'

'I'll just check with Mum and Dad!' Mandy grinned.

'Phew!' said Mrs Hope, as Mandy and James came into the kitchen. 'That's the first time your father and I have conducted morning surgery from the kitchen of this house!'

'It would have been easier to open the surgery!' Adam Hope chuckled, carefully stepping over Timothy. The tortoise was happily investigating the kitchen floor.

'Can we take Spike for a walk?' Mandy asked eagerly.

'I don't see why not,' her father replied. 'But keep him on a lead, won't you?'

'Yes, OK, Dad,' Mandy promised.

'Yes, be careful,' Emily Hope advised. 'And remember to be back in time to visit Betty in hospital.'

'No problem,' James said.

* * *

Spike kept his head low and turned well away from Mandy as she clipped a leather lead to his collar. He seemed to shudder when she touched him.

'Walkies!' she said briskly, hoping to see a flicker of interest in the dog's nervous eyes.

'Nothing!' observed James, sadly. He was used to Blackie's delight at the merest hint of an outing. 'Not even a wag of his tail.'

They set out in the direction of the Mabsons' dairy farm. The brooding clouds of the day before had gone and it was bright and very cold. Spike walked obediently beside Mandy, keeping in step with her and showing little interest in his surroundings. The tips of his coal black ears twitched and she could tell he was as tense as could be.

'He doesn't seem to be enjoying himself much,' James said. 'How can we perk him up a bit?'

'I wonder when this poor dog last had any *fun*,' Mandy said. 'I know, let's run. Come on, boy!' They broke into a jog, cresting a little rise and plunging down the snowy slope. Spike ran with them, rather miserably, his tail tucked between his legs. They sank into the snow, breaking the even surface with their boots. A twinge of pain reminded Mandy of her twisted ankle and she began to slow down.

Just then, a big buck hare broke cover from under a bush. Its smooth brown coat was stark against the white of the snow. Terrified, it streaked across their path, seeking an escape from the approaching humans and their dog.

Spike's head whipped up and, in a moment, he had pulled the lead free of Mandy's hand. He took off like a bullet, flying across the snow in pursuit of the hare.

'Spike!' Mandy yelled. '*No!* Come back!'

'Oh, *crikey*!' James moaned. 'Now we're in trouble.'

The dog loped effortlessly across the huge expanse of snow. He was far out of their reach and Mandy knew he would not respond to her call. Her heart began to hammer fearfully in her chest. The seconds ticked by as they watched helplessly – and then, suddenly, Spike seemed to vanish from sight.

'Where'd he go?' James said, puzzled. 'He's disappeared . . . like magic!'

'How strange!' Mandy gasped. 'He was there

one second and gone the next! James, quick, we've got to go and find him!'

As they ran, Mandy's mind was racing. The only explanation was that the dog had been swallowed up by a drift of soft snow – but, if that were the case, why hadn't he reappeared? James was ahead of her, following Spike's tracks. As they drew nearer the spot where he'd mysteriously vanished, the sound of splashing alerted Mandy to the dog's fate.

'Oh, no!' she shouted. 'James, he's gone through the ice. He's in the Mabsons' reservoir!'

She'd seen it in the summer. Jack Mabson had had it built to help with the irrigation of his fields. Mandy remembered its smooth stone sides, and the dark, almost black, water lapping at its circular edge. Spike must have managed to clear the fence.

The terrified dog was thrashing around in the ice that crusted the surface. There was an ominous cracking as he tried to find support for his front feet. The ice splintered and Spike clawed frantically at the sheer, moss-covered sides.

'Spike!' screamed Mandy. She kneeled in the snow, stretching out to grab the dog's collar. But he paddled sideways, just out of her reach. She

watched, horrified, as he sank, exhausted, beneath the surface of the jagged hole in the ice.

'Spike!' she shouted again. In spite of his fear, the dog still seemed reluctant to trust her.

'Don't be so stubborn!' James pleaded, as though the dog could understand. 'We're trying to *help* you!'

Again and again, Spike tried to save himself by avoiding contact with Mandy or James. He kept away from their grasping hands, stark panic showing in his eyes. He seemed to be weighing up which was the worse fate – the icy water, or the hands trying to grab at him.

Mandy felt desperate. Each time Spike sank underneath the surface of the reservoir her fear for him grew, until she was tempted to jump into the freezing water herself. She reached out a hand, straining every muscle – and this time, defeated, Spike paddled towards her and allowed her to take hold of his collar.

James grabbed two handfuls of Mandy's coat and held on as she cried, 'I've got him! Pull James, *pull*!'

The weight of the big wet dog was a surprise. He came out of the water in a rush, slivers of ice sliding off his coat. He sneezed and shivered and shook – and without even thinking, Mandy's arms came up round his shoulders in relief. She hugged him to her, her cheek pressed against his.

This time, he didn't warn her off with bared teeth, or growl. He accepted her affection, looking at her with his solemn brown eyes full of bewilderment as though, at last, he understood.

'Oh, James,' Mandy whispered, through chattering teeth. 'We've won! I really think we've won.'

* * *

Spike was encouraged to lie beside a blazing log fire in the sitting-room at Animal Ark. The wet peaks of his coat dried to a soft golden shine and he allowed Mandy to stroke him while she and James told Mr and Mrs Hope what had happened.

'Hasn't he changed?' Emily Hope said, shaking her head in disbelief. 'He's a different animal to the one you left here with just a couple of hours ago.'

'His perspective has changed,' Adam Hope suggested. 'The world he knew was a cruel place, where humans couldn't be trusted not to hurt or frighten him. Now, he knows better.'

'He's a lovely dog,' Mandy smoothed Spike's ears, which were hot from the fire. He gave a great, contented sigh, as if he couldn't quite believe his luck. 'And to think we almost lost him!'

'I must have a word with Jack Mabson about his fencing,' Mr Hope said. 'It could have been one of *you* in the reservoir!'

Mandy shuddered. It had been a horrible experience – one she wouldn't want to repeat to Betty until her friend was feeling much stronger and less worried about her animals in general.

'We'd better go now,' Mrs Hope said, glancing

at her watch. 'Or visiting hours will be over. We'll put the fireguard up, and leave Spike resting where he is, shall we?'

'What about Timothy?' James asked.

'He's doing well,' Mr Hope replied. 'He's been cruising around in the kitchen, exploring. He can't come to any harm and there's water and food for him if he decides he wants it.'

'Thanks, Mr Hope,' James said gratefully.

Spike lifted his head and looked at Mandy as she made to leave the room. A trace of anxiety flickered in his eyes.

'You stay there,' she said. 'I'm going to visit your mistress – and then I'll be back.'

Spike lay down again and closed his eyes. Somehow, Mandy knew that the edgy, mistrustful Spike was gone for ever.

Betty was sitting up in her bed on the ward she shared with several other patients. She was surrounded by vases of flowers, so Mandy was pleased she had decided on chocolates instead.

'Hmm, chocolate brazils, my favourites.' Betty grinned. 'Thanks. How are all the animals? You found Timothy all right?'

'Yes, I'm looking after him,' James said proudly, adding, 'with a bit of help from Mr Hope.'

'And Bubbles?' she prompted.

'Doing fine,' Adam Hope said with a smile, 'with Ted Forrester.'

'Chuck and Allie? Pippa and Whisky? The dogs?'

'With the Hardys,' Mr Hope nodded.

'And Spike?' Betty made a face. 'I don't expect he's let anyone near him, has he?'

'Oh, yes.' Mandy grinned. 'Spike is at home, with me. He and I are good friends now.'

'*Wow!* I can hardly believe it,' she said. She put her bandaged hand on top of Mandy's who was closest to her, and gave it a pat. 'You've been brilliant – all of you. I'm really grateful. I don't know what would have become of them all . . .' She trailed off as her eyes filled with tears. Emily Hope moved quickly and slipped an arm round her shoulders.

'There's no need to worry, Betty,' she said gently. 'All of the animals are in good hands. As soon as your barn is rebuilt, their foster families will bring them back to you.'

'Yes,' Mandy smiled encouragingly. 'The

sanctuary will be as good as new – better than new!'

'That's just it,' Betty shook her head sadly. 'There's not going to be a sanctuary. Not any more.'

'What?' said Mandy, gaping at Betty rather rudely. 'What do you mean?'

'You can't give up!' James begged. 'It's a brilliant sanctuary. You mustn't let a little thing like a *fire* put you off.'

Emily Hope held up a hand. 'Why don't we give Betty a chance to explain,' she suggested quietly.

'It's the insurance,' Betty mumbled. 'It lapsed a couple of weeks ago. I meant to fill out the paperwork to have it renewed but, I've been so busy . . .' Betty trailed off.

'Lapsed?' said Mandy, puzzled.

'I mean, I haven't got any insurance,' Betty said miserably. 'I've been so . . . foolish! Stupid!'

'Yes, well, that could be a problem,' Adam Hope looked uncomfortable.

'You mean, there isn't any money to have the barn rebuilt?' James asked.

Betty shook her head, then let it fall back against the pillow. 'Stupid! How stupid I've been!'

she repeated. There was a minute's awkward silence. Mandy allowed this latest piece of news to sink in. She could hardly believe it. Her mother kept her arm firmly round Betty's shoulders.

'Any idea how the fire started?' Mr Hope asked.

'No,' Betty mumbled. 'Only, I do know that the two men who delivered the logs were both smoking cigarettes!'

'I suppose it's possible they might have thrown a lit cigarette down and started the blaze,' Emily Hope said. 'But there's no way of proving that!'

'No,' Betty agreed sadly.

'No electrical equipment in the barn that might have been faulty?'

'No,' Betty said again.

'But . . . there must be *something* we can do!' Mandy pleaded. 'We can't just allow the sanctuary to close!'

Betty's next remark was drowned out by the sound of a nurse wheeling a trolley piled with clattering crockery on to the ward. The pungent smell of fish wafted across the room.

'Ugh,' said Betty. 'Supper. It's not terribly good here.'

'Never mind,' Emily Hope smiled. 'You'll

soon be home. We'd better go.'

'Thanks for coming,' Betty said. Her eyes were red-rimmed and Mandy could see just how wretched she felt.

She slipped over to her side. 'We'll think of something,' she whispered. 'Don't you worry. James and I will come up with a plan. Remember when we stopped Sam Western raising the rent and helped repair it? We'll do it again. There's just no way the sanctuary is closing, that's for sure!'

Eight

All through Sunday evening and most of the night, Mandy was preoccupied with a single thought: how to save the sanctuary from closing. She was well aware of just how hard Betty had struggled to afford the food, bedding and veterinary treatment for her many rescued animals as it was, even though her parents often overlooked payment for their work. With no insurance money due, and the impossibly high cost of a new barn, there seemed very little hope.

Thousands of pounds, her father had said. At least fifteen thousand – and it was this figure that occupied her thoughts as she walked Spike through Welford on Monday morning. Her fingers strayed to the top of his soft head and the big dog looked up at her gratefully. Was she imagining it, or was there a little spring in his step today?

James was shovelling snow off the paved pathway to the back door of his house when Mandy called out. 'Hi, James. Have you come up with any ideas for raising money for the sanctuary?'

'Only the most obvious ideas,' he admitted, resting his chin on the top of the spade. 'Like having a sale or something.'

'Cakes . . . books, old toys,' Mandy shrugged. 'That won't make much.'

'A raffle?' James said. 'That's another idea I had.'

'My dad says we'll need to make a lot of money – about fifteen thousand pounds,' Mandy told him.

'Oh, no.' James looked defeated as he pushed his glasses higher up the bridge of his nose with his mittened hand. He sighed heavily.

'Oh, James,' Mandy was miserable. 'All those

animals. What will become of them? There isn't any way we can raise the sort of money that's needed.'

'I can't bear to think about it. We'll just *have* to come up with something,' James reminded her, adding, 'We promised Betty we would, didn't we?'

'Do you think people would make donations?' Mandy asked.

'They might . . . but not fifteen thousand pounds worth of donations,' he reasoned.

Spike began to growl. He strained forward on the lead and Mandy wound it tightly round her hand. 'It's OK, Spike,' she soothed him. 'It's only a boy delivering the morning newspapers.'

'Newspapers!' James repeated, his eyebrows high. The boy came into the garden and skirted the big dog warily. Spike's hackles rose high.

'He won't hurt you,' Mandy reassured him, but the boy shoved his newspaper through the letter slot and scampered away without replying. As he did so, a piece of paper fluttered from his pocket and fell into the snow. Mandy picked it up.

'Newspapers,' James said again, snapping his fingers. 'We could tell them the sad story of Betty's burnt-down barn. It would make a good story – and get people's sympathy.'

'Yes! Good idea,' Mandy agreed. 'That's a start, anyway. Letting people know about what happened.' Idly, she began to read the piece of paper in her hand. It was an invitation to a charity dinner in the town hall. As she read, an idea formed in her mind.

'James!' she shouted, startling him so that he missed with his shovel and smacked it into the trunk of a tree.

'What?'

'I've had a brilliant idea!' Mandy was hopping from foot to foot in her excitement. She gabbled on: 'You know Gran and Grandad are having a huge party to celebrate their anniversary? There's going to be dancing and loads of food and everything?'

'Yes?' James looked bewildered. 'So?'

'So, my grandparents can *charge* people to come to the party! Everyone who agrees to come – and dance and drink and eat – will have to *pay*! And all the money will be donated to Betty's worthy cause!' Mandy finished, breathless and triumphant.

'I don't think your gran will like it,' James shook

his head. He looked very doubtful.

'Of course she will,' Mandy was certain. 'We'll persuade her. Let's go to Lilac Cottage right this minute and tell her she just *has* to help. After all, it's an emergency, isn't it?'

'Right,' said James hesitantly. 'We can try. Come on.' He tossed the shovel aside and fell into step beside Mandy.

When Mandy and James arrived at Lilac Cottage, Grandad was busy having a conversation with their newly-resident goat. 'I don't care if they are your favourites,' he was saying. 'Dorothy will skin you alive if you eat 'em again, is that clear?' The goat bleated disdainfully, glaring at Grandad with its yellow eyes.

'Hello, Grandad,' Mandy chuckled. 'Having trouble with her?'

'Morning, love. Hello, James.' Tom Hope grinned. 'Oh, she's a one, she is. I planted these flowers especially for your gran, right near the kitchen window so she could see them, but this goat seems determined to have the lot for a snack!'

Mandy laughed. 'Is Gran in?' She held Spike tightly, as he eyed the goat fiercely.

'Inside, making lists of food for our anniversary party,' he replied. 'She won't mind an excuse for stopping. Go on in.'

'Ooh, should you be bringing that dog in here, Mandy?' Dorothy Hope peered nervously at Spike on the front door step. 'He looks terribly cross . . . isn't he the rescue dog that Betty was having all the trouble with?'

'*Was* having trouble with, Gran, you're right. But no more!' Mandy told her proudly. 'Now, he's learned to trust people more and he's being very good.'

'Well, if you're sure,' Gran looked uncertain. 'He won't harm Jazz, will he?'

'Jazz who?' said James.

'That bird we took in,' Dorothy Hope shook her head. 'I tell you – he's a character. I'm getting used to him. But he does say some funny things.'

The cockatiel was sitting on top of his cage preening its wing feathers. It was the most handsome bird Mandy had ever seen – and the cleverest.

'Where's your wife?' it said, cocking its head as she approached, sending her into fits of giggles. Spike's nose twitched and he stretched forward

to get a closer look, but Mandy held him back.

'Gran! He's amazing! How do you know his name is Jazz?' she asked.

'Jazz is a pretty boy!' the cockatiel said.

'Well, he sort of told us!' Gran admitted. 'Of course, he may be stringing us along. He's very bright and loves teasing us.'

'Why doesn't he fly away?' James asked.

'Mind your own business,' Jazz told him and turned his back to James.

'Betty clipped his wings, by the looks of things,' Gran said, while James rocked with laughter. 'He must once have been able to fly, because he flew away from his owners. Betty didn't want to take that chance again.'

'This chap is a real character,' Grandad added, as he came into the kitchen with his boots in his hand. 'Somebody, somewhere, must be very sad to have lost this little fellow.'

'What have you done with that goat and her kid?' Gran eyed her husband suspiciously. 'You didn't leave them crunching up my . . .'

'No, Dorothy,' Grandad sighed. 'I've put them back into the shed. They'll do no more harm today.'

'Well, I wonder when poor Betty will be up and about and have that barn of hers rebuilt,' Gran said, cutting some slices of a home-made carrot cake. 'It can't really happen soon enough.'

'That's what we've come to tell you,' Mandy said. 'We went to see Betty in hospital last night and . . .'

'Her hands are all bandaged up,' James put in, staring at the butter icing on the top of the cake. Gran handed him a slice on a plate with a small fork.

'It's quite gooey,' she warned. 'How *is* Betty?'

'She's fine – well, she is, and she isn't,' Mandy said.

'What do you mean?' Grandad looked puzzled.

'Well, you know how you're supposed to have insurance so that if you have a problem the company you're insured with will give you money?' Mandy began.

'She hasn't got any insurance on the barn!' James finished. 'Not a penny. So there's no money to have another one built.'

'What?' said Gran, looking startled. 'But, why not?'

'She forgot!' Mandy announced. 'It slipped her mind, is what she said.'

'Oh, no,' Grandad muttered. 'That's not good. What's she going to do?'

'Well, that's what we wanted to talk to you about.' Mandy smiled sheepishly.

'Put a sock in it!' shouted Jazz from his perch on the top of the cage. 'Go to blazes!'

'Jazz!' Gran scolded. 'Your language! I'm sorry Mandy, love. Do go on. Your grandad and I will do anything we can to help, of course.'

'Within reason,' Grandad said firmly. 'I can't build anything, not at my age . . . not even if it *is* for a good cause.'

'No!' Mandy chuckled. 'It's nothing like that. We were wondering if . . . you would – um – consider asking your guests to pay to come to your anniversary party?'

Gran's eyebrows rose. 'How much?' she said, and took a sip of her tea.

'We hadn't worked that out, Mrs Hope,' James said, running his finger round the edge of the plate for the last trace of sweet icing.

'Actually, Dorothy,' Tom Hope grinned, after a moment's thought, 'it's not such a bad idea. People around here will be sympathetic to Betty. I'm sure nobody would object putting their hands in their pockets for a good dinner and dance.'

Gran was silent, thinking. Jazz hopped on to the back of a nearby chair and shuffled along looking interested. 'Stars and Stripes,' he said. 'Salute the Stars and Stripes!'

'There's American in that bird,' Gran said, looking thoughtful.

'Twenty pounds a couple?' said Grandad.

'How much will that make, altogether?' Mandy felt excitement begin to flow through her.

'Well, let's see now . . .' Gran reached for her notepad and a pencil. 'So far, we've had ninety acceptances. That makes . . . about eighteen hundred pounds.'

'That's not enough,' James said flatly. 'Not *nearly* enough.'

'Well, no,' Mandy agreed, 'but we can do other things as well! We can organise a raffle and tell the local newspapers to write a story and . . .'

'I'm sure people who aren't coming to the party will give generously anyway,' Gran said.

Mandy got up and hugged her Gran tightly. 'You're an angel, Gran. And you, Grandad.

Thanks for agreeing to this. It will all help, won't it?'

'It will, lass,' smiled Grandad. 'It certainly will.'

'I'll have to telephone everyone and warn them,' Gran said. 'The invitations have already gone out and I said nothing about a *fee* . . .'

'I'll help you,' Grandad said.

'We'd better go,' said Mandy. 'There's a lot to organise. James and I want to try and get in touch with the local newspaper office today.'

'How's Meadow?' Gran asked.

'She's coming on well. Simon says she's constantly hungry. I'm hoping to go and see her again today,' Mandy said, making a mental note that she must make some time for the little cub.

'I'm glad to hear it,' Gran said.

'Take it a bit easy, lass,' Grandad said, putting an arm round her and giving her a squeeze. 'You're only one wee girl. And go gently on that ankle of yours.'

'I will, Grandad.' Mandy sighed. 'But I could do without it, right now. We'll let you know how we get on.'

'Thanks for the cake,' James said, as they went out of the front door.

* * *

Spike was showing a greater interest in his surroundings on the way back to Animal Ark. As they walked along, he turned his head to watch people passing, and there was an occasional twitch in his plumy tail. Mandy decided to go to the surgery first, and visit Meadow.

She found Simon with the fox cub in his arms. She was wrapped in an old towel and sucking on her bottle. 'Ah,' breathed Mandy, 'she's so sweet!'

'Sweet – and hungry!' Simon retorted. 'She never stops!'

'I've been so busy with the animals in the house, or I would have helped you with her,' Mandy apologised.

'You've got more than enough to cope with,' Simon chuckled. 'How's young Timothy, James?'

'Hasn't eaten a bite,' James said gloomily. 'I'm really worried.'

'He'll come round,' Simon grinned. 'Honestly, don't worry.'

Mandy stroked Meadow's downy forehead and the cub stopped suckling. She pulled away from the teat and it made a little popping noise. There was a creamy tide of milk round her tiny mouth.

'Can we use the phone?' Mandy asked suddenly. There were more urgent matters to be dealt with – although she *was* reluctant to part from Meadow.

'Yes, use the one in the supplies room,' Simon suggested. 'No one will disturb you in there. Why – what are you up to?'

'We're going to tell the newspapers about Betty's barn burning down. People might ring up the paper and offer to donate some money to help rebuild it,' James explained importantly.

'That's a great idea,' Simon said. 'It's a good local story. I should think they'll send a reporter right away.'

'Really?' Mandy smiled. 'Oh, that would be great! Let's go, James.'

Mandy easily found the telephone number of the *Welford Echo* in the book. Rather nervously, she dialled and asked to speak to a reporter. Several seconds passed, while the telephone played her a little tune. Then:

'Newsdesk,' said a brisk voice. 'Can I help you?'

'Yes, please,' Mandy began. 'My name is Mandy Hope. I'm a friend of Betty Hilder, who runs the Welford Animal Sanctuary . . .'

'Oh yes, I know it,' said the voice.

'Well, it's burned down!' Mandy said. 'All the animals have been rescued by the villagers, but Betty is in desperate need of help . . .'

James made a thumbs-up sign, to show Mandy she was doing a great job.

'Can I have your name again? And your address, please?'

Mandy made the thumbs-up sign back at James as she gave her details.

'My name is Richard Harborne,' the man said. 'Thanks for letting us know. Um, I expect we'd like a photograph of one of the rescued animals. Any suggestions, Mandy?'

Mandy was grinning with delight. Her first thought was of Jazz – the amazing cockatiel. 'Yes,' she said. 'I'll give you my grandparents' address in Welford. They have a couple of Betty's animals staying there.'

Mandy gave Dorothy and Tom Hope's address and arranged a time to meet Mr Harborne at Lilac Cottage. She was sure Gran and Grandad wouldn't mind. He thanked her again and, when she'd replaced the receiver, she grabbed James

round the waist. She danced him round in a circle,
making Spike bark.

'This is going to be brilliant!' she said. 'We're
going to save the sanctuary, I just *know* we are!'

Nine

James had gone home to walk Blackie and when Mandy went into the kitchen for her lunch, she found that her mum had left a cheese and pickle sandwich on the table. Beside it was a note that read: *I've been called out to a road accident – Dad's in surgery. Please feed chinchilla! Love, Mum.*

Mandy went straight upstairs to check on her charges. Spike was close behind her. It was clear that he was not going to be parted from Mandy easily. She was just looking in on Clarice when the telephone rang. Mandy's immediate thought was that it might be Mr Harborne at the newspaper office.

'Hello?' she said, breathlessly.

'Mandy!' Mrs Ponsonby sounded desperate – more desperate than usual.

'Mrs Ponsonby?' Mandy said, taking a deep breath.

'My dear! I can't get hold of either of your parents – and I need help, right away. This is an emergency . . .'

'What's the matter?' Mandy asked, frowning.

'It's my gerbil – *Betty's* gerbil,' she said. 'It's disappeared!'

Amelia Ponsonby lived in an old Victorian mansion called Bleakfell Hall. She shared the cavernous rooms and large garden with her spoiled Pekinese dog, Pandora, and a rescued mongrel puppy called Toby. On the telephone, the old lady had sounded quite desperate, and so Mandy had decided to leave Spike in the kitchen and go up there herself. She knew Mrs Ponsonby well enough to know that her emergencies were usually quite manageable.

'I'm not very good with rodents,' she had cried.

'The thought of the creature hiding itself in my bed-sheets . . . Mandy, dear, do something, will you?'

Mandy chuckled as she cycled along the snowy lane. She could hardly feel the pain in her ankle now, though the purplish bruise still looked rather dramatic and had spread across the top of her foot. She made a bet with herself that the gerbil was where it should be, curled up cosily somewhere warm and safe. Mrs Ponsonby had probably overlooked it.

She pedalled over the bridge and through the imposing stone gateway, pausing to admire the hall's carved towers and turrets, which were prettily frosted with snow. She rang the bell at the front door, and Mrs Ponsonby herself opened it. Her plump face was pink with exertion and, for once, she was without an ornate hat.

'My housekeeper has the day off,' she gasped, tucking Pandora more firmly under her ample arm. The peke blinked at Mandy with big, watery eyes. 'No one around to help me – and I've searched high and low! What am I going to do? What will Betty think?'

Mandy stamped the snow off her boots and

stepped into the hall. She pulled off her woollen hat and shook out her hair. 'Don't worry,' she smiled reassuringly. 'I'm here to help. Hello, Pandora!' She could hear Toby yapping somewhere deep in the interior of the house.

But Mrs Ponsonby continued to wring her hands. 'I know that Mr Bell and Mr Pickard are doing a *sterling* job down at the sanctuary in Betty's absence . . . and I've seen Mr and Mrs Hardy out walking those four great dogs. It seems everyone is managing successfully – except me!'

'Now, Mrs Ponsonby,' Mandy soothed, 'please don't get upset. Where have you been keeping the gerbil?'

'Why, in my bedroom, of course!' she replied, as though it was the most obvious place for a gerbil to be. 'I had hoped to keep an eye on it, you see.'

'I see,' said Mandy, beginning to follow Mrs Ponsonby up the stairs.

Mandy began her search in the overly decorated pink bedroom. She saw that the little wire door of the gerbil's cage hung open. She raked gently through the shredded bedding and sawdust with her fingers and peered into the night nest. There was no sign of the gerbil.

'I expect it has got caught in a pipe, and will drown and start to smell – or it will chew through my electrical wires in the night and blow Bleakfell Hall to . . .'

'Calm down, Mrs Ponsonby,' Mandy smiled kindly. 'I'm sure we'll find it.' She began to think: *If I were a gerbil, and it was cold – as it is in this house – where would I go?*

'Pandora won't like it, she won't like it a *bit*. If she comes across it, it might give her a frightful turn.' Mrs Ponsonby was breathing heavily.

Mandy encouraged her to sit down. As the large lady sank into an easy chair by the window, the bedroom door smacked open and boisterous little Toby tore into the room. He ran round in circles, jumping up at Mandy in delight. She petted him and tried to calm him down, too.

'Oh! Now, Toby!' Mrs Ponsonby scolded. 'You're not allowed in the *bedroom*! You . . .'

But Toby had caught a whiff of something interesting. He trotted towards the big mahogany wardrobe, the door of which was ajar, and nosed it open.

'Oh, naughty, naughty dog!' flapped Mrs

Ponsonby, trying to get out of the chair. In a trice, Toby had found the source of the curious scent he'd picked up. It was a large pink slipper. He barked joyfully, staring at its feathery pom-pom tuft and wagging his tail.

Mandy lifted the slipper and looked inside it, while laughter bubbled up inside her. 'Here's the gerbil!' she cried happily. 'Toby has saved the day and – oh my goodness!'

'Oh my goodness?' Mrs Ponsonby repeated, struggling to her feet.

'Babies!' Mandy shrieked. 'Little pink babies, all crammed into the slipper!'

Mrs Ponsonby sat down again in a hurry and Pandora whined and paddled her short front paws. 'How many?' she asked weakly.

'Um . . . three, I think,' Mandy said. 'Oh, Mrs Ponsonby, they're lovely!'

'Really?' Mandy carried the slipper over to her chair and she looked in. 'Why, they're no bigger than . . . than *baked beans*!' she exclaimed.

'They'll grow,' Mandy said with a grin.

'I expect they will!' Her face broke into a smile. 'Do you hear that, Pandora? We've become parents! Mandy, dear, you must get your father or mother to ring me right away. I shall have to have a list of instructions on how to look after the young.'

'Fine, Mrs Ponsonby, I will,' Mandy replied, adding, 'You see, you *have* managed successfully, after all.'

'Yes,' Mrs Ponsonby drew herself up to her full height, looking proud. 'I expect I have!'

The next few days of half-term week raced by in a whirl of chores. It was just what Mandy loved best – helping animals. She and James dedicated themselves energetically to their many tasks, while spreading the word about the fire at the same time and drumming up support for Betty.

They cycled each day to the sanctuary, to spend time with the dogs in the kennels who were patiently waiting for the chance of a new home. Mandy took Spike along on these outings, and soon he began to wag his tail expectantly whenever she reached for her coat.

Ernie Bell and his friend Walter Pickard were proving themselves devoted carers while Betty was recovering. They spent long hours mucking out the stalls of the sheep and the cow, Bella, and

Charlie the ram, and kept a paternal eye on the ewe with her twin lambs – as well as caring for the cats.

James went with Mandy on a visit to the Hardys at the Fox and Goose. They helped Sara to groom Betty's long-haired dogs. They also called in on Mrs Ponsonby a couple of times.

'Honestly!' puffed James, after the first visit, 'Anybody would think she'd had those baby gerbils herself, the fuss she's making!'

When they went over to see Otis, the pot-bellied pig, and Ruby, they rescued muntjak deer, Jack Mabson told them that he had been horrified to hear from Mandy's father about the near-disaster at his reservoir. He had already set about repairing the fencing.

Mandy spent time at James's house, too, trying to coax Timothy to eat, but the tortoise was still stubbornly refusing all nourishment. And whenever there was a spare moment, they would look in on Meadow in the surgery hospital. Mandy loved her little pointed ears, and the way the cub lay back in her arms to drink from the bottle.

But her favourite time of all was being at home, in the spare bedroom at Animal Ark. Her time with Spike, Clarice, and Mystic – as she had called the lop-eared rabbit – and the other small animals, was special, because, for the meantime, they were hers. The very greatest reward for all her hard work was the look in Spike's eyes. His sadness and cowering nervousness was gone. Now, there was a positive glow of happiness in his grateful, golden eyes. It made Mandy's heart swell with pride.

Then, suddenly, it was the evening of Gran and Grandad's big anniversary party. Gran was standing on the front steps of the village hall when Mandy arrived with her parents. She was putting the finishing touches to a garland of silver and white ribbons.

'Don't you look lovely?' Mandy said, admiring her gran's lilac-flowered dress.

'Thank you, love. And just look at this!' Dorothy Hope brandished a copy of the local newspaper. 'We've made the weekly news!'

Mandy saw there was whole stack of copies of the *Welford Echo* on a small foyer table. She looked to where Gran was pointing in the open newspaper. Adam and Emily Hope looked too.

In the large photograph, Dorothy Hope smiled at the camera with Jazz the cockatiel on her shoulder. Mandy was on her left, holding Spike on his lead. James held up Timothy in his outstretched arms.

'Oh, it's come out brilliantly!' Mandy grinned. 'Fire at Animal Rescue Centre . . .' she began, reading aloud the bold headline.

'Everyone's been so good about paying to come this evening.' Gran smiled. 'I explained about the fire at the sanctuary, and some people insisted on paying even more than we'd asked for!'

'That's fantastic,' Mrs Hope commented.

'Dorothy,' Tom Hope called from the door into the hall, 'are you coming to this party, or not?'

'Just coming, dear!' Gran replied. 'Come on.' She linked her arm through her granddaughter's. 'Let's go and have some fun!'

A few of the early arrivals were drifting about the prettily decked-out hall, sampling the snacks and sipping their drinks. Soft music from the band on stage gave the party a real air of celebration.

'This is great,' Mandy approved, spotting James

in a corner. He was cramming a sausage roll into his mouth.

'There doesn't seem to be any ketchup,' he grumbled, as Mandy came up.

Mandy ignored him. 'Nobody could object to making a donation for this, I'm sure,' she said, taking in the party scene.

'My parents paid,' James told her. 'And gave a little extra too.'

'Good!' Mandy grinned.

She glanced around at all the familiar locals. She'd never seen Ernie Bell and his friend Walter Pickard so smartly dressed. Ernie looked distinctly uncomfortable and kept fiddling with the buttons on his waistcoat. Sara Hardy and Jean Knox wore evening gowns and Mr Spiller was wearing a dinner jacket. Even Claire McKay had had her hair done up in an elaborate style, which made her look much older than she was. Mandy looked down at her own dress. She wished she'd thought to ask her mother for something new, but there hadn't been time to think about shopping.

She moved around the hall, watching eagerly for people as they arrived. She couldn't resist counting the money they were making for Betty, as each couple came through the door.

'Well over a hundred pounds already,' James murmured, as though he could read her mind.

'James!' Mandy giggled. 'That's just what I was doing – adding it all up!'

Mr and Mrs McKay started dancing and Gran and Grandad followed their example. The band played 'You Are My Sunshine' and Mandy noticed that her grandfather was singing as he whirled Gran around in his arms.

She greeted the people she knew and smiled at those she didn't. Everywhere, the talk was of Betty's animals. Mandy caught the tail-ends of conversations as she wandered about with her Coke in her hand.

'He's settled so well!' Jack Mabson said. 'He's quite tame, for a muntjak.'

'Where do they originate from?' the woman he was talking to asked.

'Asia, I believe,' Mr Mabson replied.

'I'm not sure I want to part with her, now!' Jean Knox said. 'She's the prettiest rabbit, and so loving. Only, I'm not there during the day. It's not fair for her to be alone for long periods of time.'

'Of course, they're *dear* little things!' Mrs Ponsonby enthused. 'No bigger than baked beans, but growing very well in my care. Pandora doesn't object to them in the least!'

Mandy chuckled to herself as she went over to say hello to Simon. He was talking to his friend Michelle Holmes, a television and radio wildlife presenter. 'Meadow,' Simon was saying. 'It's what Mandy calls her. She's all set to join her family again.'

'Are Meadow's stitches out?' Mandy asked.

'Yes,' Simon nodded. 'Her tummy has healed up nicely. She's all set to go back to her family.'

'Oh, I'm so glad,' Mandy cried, then immediately felt sad at the thought of having to part with the little cub.

'I've not seen a cockatiel round here before,' Ted Forrester was saying to Tom Hope. 'I wonder where his owners are?'

'He really is a remarkable bird,' Tom Hope agreed. 'There's nothing he doesn't have an opinion about – and he's not shy to express it either!'

Mandy and James helped Emily and Dorothy Hope bring out the trays of hot food from the kitchen. There were murmurs of appreciation as the steaming platters were laid out and even a smattering of applause at the beautiful pink salmon. Then Mandy's grandad popped the cork on the first bottle of champagne and raised his glass. He tapped on the bottle with a teaspoon to ask for silence.

'I'm no good at making fancy speeches,' he announced. 'But I'd just like to make a toast to the best wife a man could have wished for – and to say sorry to her for allowing Betty's goat to polish off the last of her snowdrops!'

Everybody laughed and clapped, then crowded towards the table with dinner plates outstretched.

'It's going really well, isn't it?' Adam Hope slipped an arm round Mandy.

She nodded, and asked, 'Is everybody here, Dad, do you think?'

'I'd say so,' Mr Hope nodded. 'Even Sam Western, who's agreed to drop Betty's rent this month as his donation.'

'That's great news but we still need a lot for the repairs. I wonder how much we've made?' Mandy looked worried.

'I expect your gran will count it up carefully at the end. Apparently some people have been very generous and given much more than was suggested.'

'Really?' Mandy's eyes were shining with anticipation. The thought of being able to surprise Betty with a nice sum of money was wonderful.

James was over at the food table, heaping a portion of rice on to his plate. Mandy was just going over to join him there, when she saw the door at the back of the hall open. There, with a shy smile on her face stood Betty Hilder!

'Betty!' Mandy cried.

'Where?' James mumbled, spinning round, his mouth full.

She came slowly into the room, and all eyes turned towards her.

'Betty!' Dorothy Hope hurried forward and gave her a hug. 'How lovely to see you! We thought you were still in hospital.'

'I've come straight from there,' Betty smiled. 'I heard you were having a party here tonight. I'm sorry to have turned up unexpectedly but I couldn't think of a better way of having everyone together in one place – so that I could thank you all at once.'

The room became silent. 'I don't know what I would have done without you all,' Betty went on, smiling at the faces looking back at her. 'You've been so kind, putting yourselves out for my animals. I'm not sure how to thank you . . .

'I especially want to thank Mandy Hope, and James Hunter, for their incredible bravery. Without their help, on the day of the fire, several of my animals would have burned to death in that barn . . .' she broke off, her eyes filling with tears. Mandy rushed forward and put an arm round her waist.

'I'm going to try my best to have the barn rebuilt,' Betty continued, 'but it's going to be very expensive. I've got some begging to do at the bank and I've got a few things I can sell . . .'

'I'll build your barn,' a voice suddenly said. There was a murmuring as everyone looked around to identify it.

'It was Ernie!' Mandy hissed to James, who was standing next to her. A cheer went up from the crowd.

'I'll help you,' called out Walter Pickard, 'but only if Sam Western will donate some of his timber!'

'I don't see why not,' Sam Western spoke up rather gruffly. 'I'll do my bit, same as everybody else.' Mandy raised her eyebrows at her mother. Mr Western was well known for being rather mean.

'I'll offer the gerbil a permanent home,' Mrs Ponsonby offered, in a quavering voice. 'But I'm not sure I can keep all of her babies . . .'

'And we'll make some of our wonderful toffee and sell it! The proceeds will all go to Betty!' cried the Spry twins, Marjorie and Joan, in unison, getting into the spirit of things.

'No vet bills for any of Betty's animals for the next six months,' called Adam Hope, a grin on his face.

Emily Hope nodded, grinning. 'I'll second that!' she shouted.

'Hooray!' shouted Mandy, overcome with delight.

Betty looked dazed. She shook her head slowly from side to side, as if she couldn't quite believe what she was hearing.

'I knew there was a reason I came to live in Welford all those years ago,' she said. 'I must have known – instinctively somehow – that it was a village with a real heart.'

Ten

On Monday afternoon, Mandy came home from school to find her mother in the kitchen with Meadow in her arms.

'Meadow!' she cried, flinging her schoolbag on the floor and hurrying over. The cub looked up at her and tried to wriggle free. She could see the fine white scar on her belly where she'd had her operation. There was a fuzz of downy hair on her small red head. 'What's up, Mum?'

Emily Hope smiled. 'I wondered if you'd like to come with me to take Meadow back to her family?'

'Today! Is she ready to go?' Mandy asked wide-eyed.

'As ready as she'll ever be!' Mrs Hope laughed. 'I'm starting to think she'd rather stay here with us.'

'And . . . can she?' Mandy grinned, knowing what the answer would be.

'That wouldn't be fair to the cub. It's best for her not to become used to humans.' Mrs Hope was firm.

'I know,' Mandy sighed.

Mandy's mum handed her the small bundle, wrapped in a towel. 'Hold her tight, won't you, love?' she advised. 'She might be frightened by the car.'

But Meadow lay still in Mandy's arms on the journey back to the playing-field where she'd been found. She was content to chew lightly on Mandy's fingers.

'Do you think her mother will still be there?' Mandy wondered.

'I hope so,' Emily Hope said, as she turned on to the green. The four-wheel drive came to a bumpy halt. 'There,' she pointed. 'There are the nets.'

They walked briskly across the hard, icy ground

towards the goalposts at the far end of the field. Meadow's nose worked at the smell of the crisp, fresh air and she struggled to be put down.

'Not yet,' Mrs Hope warned. 'We don't want her running off.'

'Oh, look,' Mandy said. 'That's where the net was cut.'

'Yes,' her mother agreed. 'And look! There's the den!'

Frozen grass and weed partially hid the entrance to the foxhole, which had been dug perilously close to the net. Mrs Hope went down on her knees and peered inside.

'It smells used,' she announced, 'sort of fresh and earthy. I think Meadow's family must still be here. Put her down, let's see what she does now.'

Very gently, Mandy lowered the little cub to the ground beside the hole. She sniffed at the earth, and wobbled uncertainly on her tiny legs. Then she caught the scent of something familiar. Her nose went up, quivering, and her tail shot out behind her. She scampered down the dark entrance to her home and was out of sight in a second.

'She's gone!' said Mandy, relieved and disappointed all at once.

'We'll wait here for a bit, just in case,' Mrs Hope suggested. Mandy followed her mother's example and moved away from the den, to a distance where they could clearly see the entrance. They waited, but Meadow didn't reappear.

'Well, that's good,' Emily Hope said.

'She's well, and she's safe,' Mandy agreed. 'I love it when it all works out this way!'

'Me too,' Mrs Hope said. 'Now . . . any homework?'

Mandy pulled a face. 'Yuck. Yes,' she nodded.

'Then, let's go home, shall we?'

'I can't believe it!' said Betty, flinging her car keys on to the kitchen table. James froze, not having noticed her come into the room at all. The knife he was using to butter the sandwiches was poised in the air. It was Saturday lunch-time, and Mandy and James were helping out at the sanctuary.

'What's the matter, Betty?' Mandy looked concerned. She had to raise her voice above the sound of Ernie's persistent hammering outside. The new barn was beginning to look very respectable.

'I've been in to do battle with the council – about

this letter I got this morning!' Betty said furiously, waving it about. 'Walton Council has decided that I have to comply with the regulations for animal housing. That means the new barn will have to have all sorts of special cages, and proper heating . . . and ventilation and . . .' Betty sank into a chair, looking defeated. She put her chin in her hands.

'But that's going to cost even *more* money!' Mandy wailed.

'Precisely.' Betty looked cross. 'I've only just about managed to scrape up the funds for the barn as it is – with the help of everyone in Welford – and now *this*!'

At the tone of Betty's voice, Blackie put his nose in the palm of James's hand and one of Betty's dogs propped his nose on her knee. Mandy's hand strayed to the top of Spike's head. He was never far away from her.

Three weeks had passed since the evening of Gran and Grandad's party. It had been a stunning success and everyone was still talking about it. Betty's unexpected arrival at the party had prompted a generous response – and more money had been raised than Mandy had ever dreamed was possible.

Soon afterwards, Sam Western had delivered several truckloads of good timber from his forestry supplies and Ernie Bell, Walter Pickard, David Gill and Jack Mabson had lent a hand to clear the rubble and start the rebuilding. It seemed that everyone in the village had contributed something. Farmer Jones from Sunrise Farm donated bales of hay and straw for bedding; Mr Adams from the hardware store offered unlimited supplies of nails, paints and brushes, and even Mrs Ponsonby turned up with a collection of potted climbing plants from her greenhouse.

'For the spring,' she had said. 'To make it look more attractive.'

With Welford united in its effort to have the sanctuary rebuilt, it had looked to Mandy as though it was actually going to be possible. Until now!

'This is awful!' she groaned. 'How much extra is it going to cost?'

'Another several thousand pounds,' Betty said, in a subdued voice.

'That's ridiculous!' James exploded. He was buttering bread furiously, having glanced out of the window and seen Ernie Bell patting his stomach to make a point. 'Have you got any cheese, Betty?'

'In the fridge,' Betty said distractedly.

Mandy's mind was turning circles. They'd all worked so hard – and Betty had even had to sell her grandmother's beautiful engagement ring to make up the money needed. Now that Mandy and James were back at school, and exams were looming, she didn't know how they could devote any more time to the sanctuary, and its animals, than they were already doing. She sighed heavily. 'Oh, no,' she said. 'This is awful.'

James was slicing squares of yellow cheese from a big block. He slipped a piece into his mouth and nudged up his glasses with his forearm. 'Mr Wakeham said we had to take our collection box away from the school reception desk,' he said gloomily. 'He said three weeks was long enough for people to put money in it.'

'Yes,' Betty agreed, putting the kettle on. 'I agree with him. Everyone has been *more* than generous, already.'

Mandy's heart went out to Betty. She looked as if she was at the end of her tether. Just then, the dogs clustered around in the kitchen began to prick up their ears. Spike growled.

'Probably someone arriving to do a bit of building,' Mandy said brightly, trying to cheer up Betty. She looked out of the window. 'Um . . . no . . . it's a car I haven't seen round Welford before, Betty. A very . . . *smart* car!'

James and Betty joined her at the kitchen window. A sleek, silver Jaguar came to a stop in the drive. In the front passenger seat, a blonde-haired woman was peering around her. She looked lost.

'I wonder who it could be,' Betty said.

All three of them, accompanied by the six dogs, hurried for the door.

'Those sandwiches ready yet?' Ernie bellowed, from the top of his ladder. James pretended not to hear him. He was staring at the couple getting out of the beautiful car.

'Gosh,' whispered Mandy. 'What do you think they want?'

The woman wore an expensive full-length coat and her wrists and ears were decorated with large diamonds. Her suede boots were high heeled. The man was immaculate in a snow-white suit and fur-lined jacket.

'Well,' said Betty quietly, leaning against the door frame, 'they haven't come to offer a home to a *piglet*, that's for sure!' Betty had her hand on Spike's collar. He was still growling, but holding his bark in check.

'Is this the . . . um, sanctuary?' the woman called, trying to keep Betty's dogs at bay by holding out hands with perfectly manicured fingernails. She spoke in an American accent.

'It is!' Betty said cheerfully. 'How can I help you?'

'Donaldson's the name,' said the man, 'Bunty and Bill Donaldson. You must be Ms Hilder?'

'I am,' Betty frowned, puzzled. Mr Donaldson smacked the palm of his hand with a rolled-up newspaper. 'Ha! Didn't I tell you we'd find the place, honey?' he said triumphantly.

Bunty Donaldson ventured forward. 'We've come for Jeremiah,' she smiled. 'We're so grateful to you for taking care of him.'

Mandy could see that Betty was quickly, silently, sorting through the names of all of her many rescued animals. But she looked blank. 'Jeremiah?' she asked.

'Oh, you *have* got him, haven't you?' the woman

wailed. 'Why, it says right here is this little old country newspaper that you found him and . . .'

Mr Donaldson was leafing through the pages of the *Welford Echo*.

Mandy had a sudden thought. 'You mean Jazz?' she interrupted, smiling. 'The talkative cockatiel?'

Mrs Donaldson nodded, relief flooding her face. 'Yes, that sounds like Jeremiah,' she said.

Betty laughed. 'We call him Jazz,' she said. 'We didn't know his name. In fact – he calls *himself* Jazz!'

'That's him!' said Bill Donaldson. 'That bird never *could* say Jeremiah!'

'Is my baby all right?' his wife asked.

'Perfect!' Betty grinned. 'He's in the sitting-room,' she pointed. 'Giving everyone who comes in a very hard time!'

Everyone laughed. 'He's a very special bird,' Mrs Donaldson explained. 'He usually lives with us in London, but we couldn't bear to leave him behind when we came up here on holiday. Then, Jeremiah escaped.'

'He's been great fun,' Betty told them. 'And he's had a little holiday of his own over at Mandy's grandparents' home while I was away following the fire,' she added pointing to Mandy.

'We're so grateful,' Bunty Donaldson said again as she followed Betty into the house, stepping carefully in her high heels.

Jeremiah was sitting in his favourite spot on the back of the armchair facing the window. He cocked his head as the door opened and blinked one eye.

'And what time do you call this?' he shrieked. He ducked his head as if squaring up for a fight.

Betty and Mandy burst into giggles and James doubled over with laughter.

'Baby!' breathed Mrs Donaldson, hurrying forward. 'I've missed you!'

The bird hopped up on to her shoulder and took hold of the diamond earring in his beak. 'Now . . . baby,' she warned.

'Put a sock in it!' the cockatiel said cheekily.

'That's our boy!' grinned Mr Donaldson happily. He put his hand into the top pocket of his jacket and extracted a small envelope. 'Ms Hilder,' he drawled, taking her hand and pumping it up and down warmly. 'This is just a little something to thank you for taking care of old Jerry boy.'

Betty took the envelope he handed her, looking a little dazed. 'Thank you,' she said. 'But there's really no need to . . .' She trailed off, shrugging at Mandy and James.

Bunty Donaldson had persuaded Jeremiah through the opening of his cage and on to the perch. 'We'll bring this back real soon,' she said, as she shut the door on the bird. 'The minute we get Jeremiah safely back where he belongs, I'll have it sent over to you.'

'Close the door!' Jeremiah said, scuffling up and down the perch.

'We'll miss him, won't we?' Betty smiled at Mandy and James. They nodded.

'Goodbye, Jazz – I mean, Jeremiah,' Mandy added. The cockatiel looked back at her solemnly.

James stood watching the Jaguar going slowly down the drive, until Ernie's pleas for food got his attention. He turned to hurry back to his sandwich-making, when Betty gave a gasp and shouted with joy.

'Wow!'

'What?' Mandy had taken hold of Betty's upper arm. 'What is it?'

'It's five thousand pounds, that's what it is!' Betty screamed. *'Five thousand pounds!'*

With Mr and Mrs Donaldson's donation, Betty was able to make sure the council regulations were met. The new barn became grander with each passing day, as smart new stainless steel enclosures arrived for the animals. A local building firm had provided scaffolding and a couple of labourers, as their donation. Mandy looked forward to the weekends, when she would spend hours helping with the finishing touches to the new-look sanctuary. Visiting as often as she did made parting with Scamp and Susie, Clarice, Mystic, and the other small animals, less difficult than it might have been.

Spike seemed to miss being at Animal Ark with her. Whenever she turned up at Betty's gate on her bike, he raced down the driveway to greet her. Betty could hardly believe that he was the same quivering, aggressive dog she had tied up in the barn on the day of the fire. Now, Spike went along with Mandy, James and Blackie on regular walks. His tail thumped and swayed along with the Labrador's and if he quivered, it was from excitement rather than fear.

The new sanctuary smelled of sawdust and raw pine, and there was infrared heating and proper lighting too. Bubbles took to his new stable right away. It was roomier than his old one, and he no longer had to share it with Rosie, who was prone to loud braying at all hours of the night.

Amelia Ponsonby kept the gerbil she had christened Charmer, but returned the weaned litter of three to Betty. 'I haven't the time for so many of them,' she explained. 'I'm a very busy woman, you know.'

'There'll be homes for them somewhere,' Betty had said. 'Come the spring, there will be good homes for most of the animals, I'm sure.'

A few days later, Mandy was playing with the ferrets and James was grooming Bubbles for Betty. Suddenly he gave a shout.

'It's gone!'

'What's gone?' Mandy looked up.

'That piece of celery!' James shouted, pointing, a look of astonishment on his face.

'*Timothy's* celery?' Mandy asked, coming over.

'He must have eaten it!' James said. Together

they peered suspiciously into Timothy's enclosure. As they watched, the little tortoise fixed his beady eyes on a sliver of lettuce, opened his mouth wide, shuffled forward and snapped it up.

'Oh wow!' yelled James. 'Great! Timothy's eating! At last!' He jumped about happily, while the tortoise moved steadily from one morsel to the next. He ate and he ate, until he had polished off his entire supply of greens.

Mandy couldn't stop laughing. Her friend's tremendous relief – and the sight of Timothy gobbling up food as though he'd only just discovered it – made her roll around clutching her sides with laughter.

'It's all turned out so well!' she said, when at last she got her breath back. 'Betty's got her new sanctuary, Meadow's gone back to her home, and so has Jeremiah, Spike is a new dog – and now Timothy's eating too!'

'Our work is done!' James sighed.

'It'll never be done, James,' Betty said quietly. Mandy and James looked up, surprised. They hadn't heard Betty come into the barn. She was leaning up against the door, looking in on them.

'There will always be animals in need of help.

But, as long as there are people like you two in the world, there will also always be hope for them,' she said.

Mandy went over and gave her a hug. 'Do you like your new sanctuary?' she asked.

'It's bigger, brighter and yes, it's *better* than ever!' Betty hugged her back. 'Thanks to you two!'